Sherlock Academy

WRITTEN AND ILLUSTRATED BY

F.C. Shaw

To Stevie
& F C Shaw
2010

To Michael,
My own Watson,
And comrade in all our adventures
With Love

Table of Contents

Sherlock Academy

FINE SLEUTHS

London, England
Friday, 27 June

Rollin E. Wilson:

It is our pleasure to inform you of
your eligibility for the Sherlock
Academy of Fine Sleuths. We believe
you possess the qualities we seek in
fine students. You are invited to a
special orientation at which any
questions you have will be addressed.

Please take advantage of our taxi
service that will pick you up on
Tuesday, 1 July at 8:00 am. We
request you bring only the following
item: your favorite book.
We anticipate making your acquaintance.

CHAPTER 1

An Invitation

The letter arrived by courier during breakfast.

"Go on, Rollie, read it aloud to us." Mrs. Wilson nudged his shoulder. She blinked at him with motherly patience radiating on her rosy face.

Rollie stared at the letter in hand, his brown eyes wide with excitement.

"Who would send him mail?" Edward, an older twin brother, snorted.

"I don't even get mail and I have a girlfriend," Stewart, the other twin, added.

"Maybe that's it!" Edward exclaimed, grinning his famous lopsided smile. "Got a secret girlfriend, Rollie? I'll bet it's Cecily Brighton!"

"I wish I'd get a letter," Lucille, a younger twin, pouted.

"Me too!" Daphne, her twin, chimed.

"Find a boyfriend and you'll get mail," Edward quipped.

Stewart slapped a high-five with his twin. The two teens snickered and elbowed each other.

"Stop it, boys. Let Rollie read it aloud," Mrs. Wilson scolded as she tenderly brushed Rollie's sandy-blond hair with her fingers.

Rollie cleared a dry throat unnecessarily. In a high voice common to boys of ten years, Rollie read the letter aloud. When finished, the entire Wilson family started talking at once with high-handed opinions, as was their custom.

"Whoever heard of the Sherlock Academy?"

"Why Tuesday?"

"It's the first of the month."

"I want a letter!"

"Me too!"

"Get a boyfriend."

Amidst all the banter around the breakfast table, Rollie sat silently, regarding his hash browns, the only food he ate for breakfast. His mind spun with questions. His middle fluttered with butterflies. He felt that flutter only three times a year: on his birthday, on Christmas day, and on the first day of school. Most children his age became very hyper when they felt this flutter in their middles. Perhaps they nagged their parents to no end, or galloped around the house squealing, or did something really naughty like peek at their presents. But in the Wilson household, there was never need for Rollie to behave this way. Everyone else was louder or more hyper, which oddly enough calmed him. Such was the case at the breakfast table laden with pancakes and eggs.

Rollie folded the letter and tucked it in his brown trouser pocket. As he tuned out everyone's comments, he noticed one family member not contributing an opinion. He threw a sideways glance at his great-auntie Ei, who got bothered by everyone, yet understood him. She sat primly, sipping her tea and holding her tongue.

He picked up his fork and poked his hash browns. He scooped up a bit, brought it to his nose, and sniffed. Nope, no use eating at a time like this. Whenever he found that flutter, his appetite vanished until the excitement resolved. Maybe it was good he got that flutter only three times a year, otherwise he might be even skinnier.

Rap-rap-rap!

Mr. Wilson rapped his knuckles on the table, the only method to get attention. "Enough, enough! I will lay out the facts and there will be no more talk of this until Tuesday."

Mr. Wilson taught mathematics at the local Technical College and loved facts as much as he hated speculation. He embodied a professor in his tweed suit, perched spectacles, and straight-combed hair. "Fact: this letter is addressed to Rollie, so it follows that it's no one else's business." He gave a warning eye at Lucille and Daphne who were uncommonly nosey for seven year olds. "Fact: the orientation will answer all our questions. Fact: the orientation is not until Tuesday. Fact: there is nothing we can do until Tuesday. Fact: this conversation is summed."

Mr. Wilson stood from the table and marched out of the dining room, his morning paper tucked under his arm.

"The day has started." Mrs. Wilson also stood, smoothing her blue print dress. "Edward, Stewart, your lunches are in the kitchen. Don't be late today or you just might get fired. Girls, you have dance lessons at nine. Auntie Ei, Toby will drive you to your bridge club at--"

"I know, Eloise. Do not boss me around like one of your brood!" Auntie Ei rose briskly to her feet and scuttled away despite her eighty-odd years.

"Rollie, your violin lesson is cancelled today. Mrs. Trindle has taken ill." She smoothed his sandy-blond hair and nudged him on his way.

Rollie smiled as the family dispersed. He cared less for violin lessons than when he first begged Mrs. Wilson for them. He had wanted to play the violin for the sole purpose of mimicking Sherlock Holmes. He enjoyed playing the violin fine, but he disliked Mrs. Trindle. She smelled stale and flicked the underside of his wrists to "improve the posture", so she said. No violin lesson meant no other plans for the whole day, which spelled freedom until suppertime. *Ahh,* summer days.

Lots of time also overwhelmed him. What to do? His brain ran through all the things he loved doing.

Play chess? Hmm…he stared around the empty parlor. Not a very fun game against himself.

Draw a map of the Wilson manor? Naw, he had done that too many times and was sure he could do it from memory easily. No challenge there.

Spy on his new next-door neighbor Mr. Crenshaw? Yeah, that could be fun. Oh wait—Rollie remembered overhearing the old man tell his secretary he would be in the city today.

Finish reading *Robinson Crusoe?* Sure. It was a good summer read since the setting was a tropical island out in the blue. At first the book had sailed Rollie far across the ocean to palm trees and warm beaches. Recently, it had grown a bit dull. Not one of his favorite books—

Favorite book!

Rollie raced up the stairs two at a time, pulling himself up by the polished banister. At the end of the hall on the second floor, he mounted twelve more stairs leading to the top of the house. He flew into his bedroom opposite the attic. Being the middle child with no twin did have its advantages: his own bedroom. Though the smallest bedroom in the large house, it belonged to him. He knew if Auntie Ei did not live with them, he would occupy her spacious room, but he never voiced this for fear of hurting her feelings.

Auntie Ei was a lady of property. Long ago, she had passed down the Wilson manor to Rollie's father as an early inheritance on the condition that she would live with them. This meant an unpleasant addition to the family and a small room for Rollie. Never mind, Rollie loved his little room, which resembled a watchtower. It had one window overlooking Mr. Crenshaw's garden—great view for spying. Best of all, he was allowed to keep his room any way he wanted.

On the wall nearest the window, he had covered the surface with cork to tack up clues and notes from the cases he solved. On his desk below the window, a telescope peeked through, kept company by a magnifying glass, a spyglass, and binoculars—he had every occasion to use them all. The rest of his room was filled with boyish delights like a BB rifle, a model airplane, a pennant of his favorite rugby team, and books and books and books.

Rollie plopped down on the navy carpet next to his bookcase. He did not organize his books alphabetically by author or title or even topic like the family's private library downstairs. Instead he organized them by personal rating. Stuck to each shelf, a little label explained his rating system.

The top shelf's label read in his best handwriting *Excellent Books, My Favorites*. The shelf below said *Good Books I Like*. Below that, *Okay Books That Were Sort of Good*. The last shelf read *Books I Didn't Really Like*. The only reason he bothered to keep the books on this last shelf was for appearances only—he hated empty bookshelves. Too lonely. The books on all the shelves constantly shuffled around as he read new ones and added them, or re-read some and revised his rating.

Running his finger along the spines on the top shelf, he read each title lovingly, mental pictures from the stories hugging his mind. Great characters paid their respects: Tom Sawyer, Robin Hood, Peter Pan, Lancelot, Sherlock Holmes—

Rollie slid out one of four volumes: *The Return of Sherlock Holmes.* He opened the green hardcover and flipped through the worn book to *The Adventure of the Empty House.* These pages preserved smudges and creases from countless reads. This was his favorite story. He smiled as he dog-eared the page and set it aside for Tuesday.

But…he fished out the letter from his pocket and read it again.

We request that you bring only the following item and nothing else: your favorite book.

What he picked out was his favorite *story.* That was okay; when it came down to it, the whole volume was his favorite too. When he thought more about it, he was not sure about bringing a Sherlock Holmes volume. Would every other student bring one also, since they were visiting the *Sherlock* Academy? Maybe the school would frown upon that, thinking he brought it in hopes of being accepted.

He scanned the top shelf again. Maybe a different book. He had other favorite books.

No.

Sherlock Holmes remained his ultimate favorite. He revered that detective; Holmes was his hero. He got teased about that.

"He doesn't have any special powers," Edward had pointed out.

"He has the power of deductive reasoning," Rollie had argued.

"Any human can have that," Edward had snorted. "Can he fly or stop a moving train? Does he even have muscles?" Edward had struck a pose in attempts to show off his sinewy muscles outlining his tall, lean body. "No? Not a hero to me then."

"He's smarter than Superman," Rollie had insisted.

"What does that matter?"

Rollie did not care about his brother's opinion. He knew Holmes was a worthy hero. Holmes did have muscles, for he was exceptional in boxing and fencing. He could disguise himself, identify all types of cigar and pipe ash, and solve any mystery simply by observing and reasoning. Rollie wanted to be just like him.

Maybe this academy would show him how…if that was what it was all about. No way of knowing until Tuesday. He leaned against his bed and flipped open the volume again. He started reading his favorite case for the umpteenth time, just to refresh his memory in case they quizzed him about it on Tuesday.

"Hallo, Rollin Holmes!"

Rollie snapped his head up from his book. "Hallo, Cecily Watson."

"Which one are you reading?" Cecily bounced into the room, her curly auburn ponytail bobbing around her shoulders. She wore a pair of brown slacks too big for her, the legs rolled up above her ankles and the waist scrunched by a belt to keep them up. She wore a green cardigan with a little patchwork bird on one shoulder. "Wait, let me guess. Give me some clues."

"Books."

"Clue."

"Uh, book seller."

"One more clue."

"House."

"*The Adventure of the Empty House*," Cecily announced triumphantly. "Although I should have guessed from the beginning— it's your favorite. I love *The Adventure of the Dying Detective.* Brilliant!"

"Did you steal your brother's trousers again?"

Cecily wrinkled her nose peppered with freckles. "Yeah. Mum still won't buy me my own pair. She says it's not lady-like."

"It's not."

"But I can't climb fences and crawl through bushes and spy in a dress," she pointed out.

"Mr. Crenshaw is in London today, remember?"

"I know. Oo, which reminds me! The Telegram Case…"

"Was it German?"

"Yes. There's another case wrapped, Holmes." Cecily pulled out a small pocket-notebook and a stubby pencil from her back pocket.

Rollie reached over and grabbed the same from his desk. They both flipped through a few pages of notes, then scratched check marks next to *Telegram Case,* found at the bottom of a long list of cases they had solved so far that summer.

Cecily paused, narrowing her eyes at him, thinking very carefully.

"What?" Rollie narrowed his eyes back at her.

"I have a secret."

"Me too."

"At least I think it's a secret."

"Me too."

"I want to tell you because you're my best friend."

"Me too."

"For goodness' sake, Rollie, stop copying me."

Rollie grinned. "I'm not. I really have a secret. I want to tell you too. I think I can. I mean, I wasn't told not too."

"Me too, but it's more intriguing if you're secretive about it."

"I agree. So tell me."

Cecily shook her head, her ponytail whipping her rosy cheeks. "You tell me yours first."

"But you mentioned your secret first."

"Oldest to youngest."

"Cecily, I'm only two months older than you."

"It still counts."

"Nope, ladies first."

"I'm not a lady we decided." She shoved her hands deep into the trouser pockets. "Tell me or I'll call you Roly-Poly."

"I hate that. It's not even close to my name or my nickname. My nickname is *Rollie* with a short *o*. Not *Rolie* with a long *o*."

"Roly-Poly, Roly-Poly—"

"Wait!" Rollie held up his hand. "I know how we can settle this. Let's both tell each other at the same time. In code."

"Great."

They concentrated quietly, writing in their notebooks. Then they tore off their papers and exchanged them. They used a common cipher: a long strand of letters, only every third letter used to make words. Quickly they circled every third letter, read the remaining letters, then gaped at each other.

"You got a letter too?" Cecily gasped.

"It came this morning!"

"Mine too!"

"What's your favorite book you're bringing?" Rollie eyed her.

"Um, the least of my questions right now. How about this question: what is this all about?" Cecily yanked out her letter from a back pocket. "I've never heard of this Sherlock Academy of Fine Sleuths."

"It's really exciting."

"I'm not so sure yet. It could be a fraud."

Rollie blinked at her. The thought that the academy might be illegitimate never crossed his mind. He was too enraptured by the idea of becoming a sleuth. Leave it to Cecily to call him back to earth. "Are you going?"

Cecily shrugged. "I suppose so. There's nothing to lose, but I'm not getting my hopes up. My mum says I can go, so that's good. At first she thought it would be too much trouble, but then she read they would pick me up."

"Where is it, do you think?"

"The return address says London."

"That's not much to go on. London's huge."

Cecily stood and paced the bedroom. "Jot down the Five Ws."

Rollie flipped to a new page in his pocket-notebook. He listed down the page WHO, WHAT, WHERE, WHEN, and WHY. "Who is it?" he mumbled, scribbling. He chewed on his pencil.

"What is it?" Cecily stopped long enough to ask this question, then resumed pacing.

"Where is it? When does this academy start?"

Cecily stopped pacing and narrowed her eyes again. "Why do they want us?"

Rollie read his letter, "We believe you possess the qualities we seek in fine students."

"What qualities?"

Rollie nodded his agreement and jotted that question down. "Tuesday seems like forever away."

"Four days if you count today."

Rollie shook his head. "Let's not. Let's say three days. It's more bearable."

Cecily nodded. "Very well. Three days until we clear up this mystery."

CHAPTER 2

Taxied Away

Dinner with the Wilsons was more chaotic than breakfast because everyone wanted to share about the day. Usually Mr. Wilson told a funny anecdote about one of his students. Stewart rambled on about his sweet girlfriend Alice, whose father he worked for. Meanwhile, Edward badgered his brother's girlfriend in jealousy, stating he wanted to find a new job. Lucille and Daphne giggled about dance lessons. Auntie Ei never said a decent word. Mrs. Wilson refereed the dinner table, nudging Rollie to eat more, laughing at Mr. Wilson's story, and shushing the twins when she thought their turns were up. As for Rollie, he usually sat quietly, taking in everything, but not eating much, being a picky eater.

But tonight was different. It was Monday night, which meant Tuesday came at dawn. For the first time in awhile, the family conversation focused on Rollie and his letter. It was still chaotic.

"Tomorrow's the day, son," Mr. Wilson stated plainly in between bites of his roast beef. "Fact: it's supposed to be a beautiful day. And it's supposed to be Tuesday all day." He gave a wink.

Rollie appreciated his father's silly sense of humor.

"What time are you leaving, son?"

"Eight o'clock—"

"Eight o'clock!" Edward exclaimed. "Wait a minute. Just because that's the same time I have to leave for work doesn't mean I'm taking Roly-Poly with me. I have—"

"Edward, slow down," Mrs. Wilson cut in, buttering her roll. "Did we ask that of you and Stewart? I don't recall."

"I'm just throwing it out there before you get any ideas," Edward said, shoveling mashed potatoes into his mouth.

Stewart swallowed his bite of carrots. "Good job, Ed. Way to think ahead."

"Actually, we do need to discuss tomorrow morning." Mrs. Wilson dabbed her mouth with a napkin. "We haven't decided who is going with Rollie."

"Is someone supposed to go with him?" Mr. Wilson glanced over his spectacles at her.

"Well, you didn't think he'd go alone to who knows where?"

"Roly-Poly's never been anywhere alone, have you?" Edward teased.

"I have too!" Rollie suddenly felt defensive. "I go to school alone everyday."

Stewart chuckled. "Good comeback, Rollie."

Mr. Wilson took off his spectacles and gnawed on one of the ends thoughtfully. "I can't go. I've got Mathematics 102. Eloise?"

"I can go, I suppose—"

"No, you can't, Mummy!" Daphne piped up.

"Remember, Mummy?" Lucille squealed.

"Oh, that's right!" Mrs. Wilson touched her forehead. "The girls have a morning tea at Mrs. Chester's. It's a mother-daughter thing. Boys, maybe—"

"Mu-um!" both Edward and Stewart whined at the same time.

"I'll accompany him." Auntie Ei stood from the table decidedly. Her tall, round figure loomed over them. "Be ready at the door at eight o'clock sharp, Rollin. That's what the letter instructed." With that, she vacated the dining room.

A few moments of unusual silence followed as the family gaped after the old woman.

Mrs. Wilson blinked. "Bless her."

Mr. Wilson grunted. "Fact: she's unpredictable."

Edward and Stewart slapped high-fives.

Lucille and Daphne giggled.

And Rollie smiled to himself, then frowned as he felt that flutter in his middle again.

*   *   *   *

As expected, Rollie's sleepless night was wrought with anxiety. That flutter in his middle never warranted a decent night's sleep. However difficult falling asleep was, somehow Rollie always woke up in the morning, which meant he had at some point indeed fallen asleep. It was mysterious.

Such was the case Tuesday morning. He was shocked to find himself waking up when his red alarm clock rang. He clicked it off and jumped out of bed. Just as he contemplated his wardrobe and panicked over what to wear (it had not crossed his mind), his mother poked her head into the room.

"Good morning, my Rollie, are you excited?"

"What should I wear, Mum?"

Clearly panic showed in his eyes and a quiver vibrated in his voice because Mrs. Wilson flitted into the room and held him close. "Don't worry. I know just the thing." She rummaged through his closet and pulled out his best blue blazer. "Wear the blue slacks and a collared shirt. Oh, and a little tie. You should look your best, I think."

Rollie did not care to dress up, but he had a feeling his mother was right. Within ten minutes he was completely dressed and groomed. Book in hand, he skipped downstairs. He had decided on *The Return of Sherlock Holmes*. Standing beside the front door, Auntie Ei leaned on her umbrella. She too was dressed nicely in a floral dress, matching hat, and white gloves. She smelled of lavender.

"Good morning, Auntie."

"Good morning, Rollin. Do you have your favorite book?"

Rollie held it up. "Think it's okay to bring a Sherlock Holmes volume?"

"Absolutely. Why not?"

"Don't you think a lot of the other kids will bring Sherlock Holmes?"

"Whoever said there would be other kids?"

Hmm, true. "Cecily is coming."

"Is she bringing Sherlock Holmes too?"

Rollie shrugged. "I don't think so."

"Well, there you have it. Straighten your tie. Don't forget your manners."

"Yes, Auntie."

Ding-Dong!

Rollie jumped. His heart skipped and his middle flipped into double fluttering. Both the parlor grandfather clock and the front doorbell chimed at the same time.

Auntie Ei opened the door to a short, squat man in a bowler hat and long black coat.

"'Morning, mum. I'm 'ere for a Rollin E. Wilson," he greeted, reading the name from an index card.

"We're ready. Rollin!" Auntie Ei called as she stepped onto the porch.

"*We*, mum? I'm just 'ere for Rollin E. Wilson."

"This is he." Auntie Ei nudged Rollie forward.

The man in black nodded curtly. "Do you intend to come along, mum?"

"I do. Is there a problem with that?"

"Depends, mum, on yer name."

"Eileen B. Wilson," she answered with meaning.

"My apologies, Lady Wilson. Let me 'elp you into the cab." He escorted Auntie Ei by the arm to a black horse-drawn cab, much like the ones popular in London in the late 1800s. It balanced on two wheels and was hitched to a single chestnut horse.

Auntie Ei seemed not the least surprised, but Rollie gaped at it, his eyes wide and his mouth open.

"You don't have an automobile?" he asked.

"No, lad, this is our taxi service." He opened two little doors that swung aside like window shutters for them and helped Auntie Ei into the cab. "This 'ere is called a hansom and it's been in the family for years. It's just like one of the hansoms—"

"Sherlock Holmes may have ridden in!" exclaimed Rollie.

"Rollin, do not interrupt. Get in," Auntie Ei ordered.

Rollie leaped into the hansom and sat on the edge of the cushion, peering out the little round window in the back. The driver climbed up to his perch above in the back, flicked the reins, and got the cab moving down the street.

"Auntie, have you ever been in one of these?"

"To answer would be to reveal how old I am. A lady never reveals her age, nor should little boys raise the question." She paused, a tight smile playing on her wrinkled face. "Perhaps I have been in one before."

Rollie expected to stop a few doors down to pick up Cecily, but the cab passed by her house. He wondered about this for a moment, but when he glanced out the window, he spotted a similar hansom and driver stopped at Cecily's house.

Within twenty minutes, they drove south into London. Normally it took ten minutes by auto. They turned down several busy streets; cars honked at the antique cab, but did not seem to bother the driver or the horse. At first Rollie knew where they were, for he visited London with his mother almost every Saturday to check the post and do a bit of shopping. As the hansom turned onto smaller streets, Rollie lost his bearings. They drove through a part of London he had never visited. Just when Rollie thought he could not be more lost, the driver pulled on the reins to stop the cab. The driver hopped off his high perch and opened the doors facing the horse. He escorted Auntie Ei down onto the sidewalk. Rollie stepped out and stared up at a tall rust brick building with rows of windows and one door. A flat roof with a chain-link fence crowned the four-story building.

"Rollie!"

Rollie whirled to find Cecily hopping out of her horse-drawn hansom. She was alone. She rushed up to him, excitement in her green eyes.

"Have you ever been in one of those cabs?" she asked him.

"No, but I really felt like—"

"Sherlock Holmes! I know! Rollie, look where we are!"

Rollie looked up again at the drab building. Posted above the mailbox next to the front door was the building's address:

221 Baker Street.

CHAPTER 3

Just Like Old Times

"*Is* this really 221 Baker Street?"

"Of course it is, Rollin, you can see for yourself on the wall." Auntie Ei ushered him toward the front double-doors.

"So this is really where Sherlock Holmes lived?"

"At one point in his life," a voice from inside answered as they bustled into the building.

They stood in a hall with a flight of stairs ascending before them. Dull green carpet spread down the hall and up the stairs. A dated gas lamp hung from the ceiling, glowing antique light on the creamy walls and dark-paneled doors. The voice emitted from a tall thin woman standing before them at the foot of the staircase. She wore a pink tie, a brown skirt, and matching blazer, which outlined her rigid posture. Her red lipstick accentuated her perfect white teeth. Her mousey-brown hair was pulled back in a tight bun. She drummed her red fingernails on the dark wooden banister.

"You will recall that Holmes' original residence was burned by his nemesis Moriarty when Holmes fled in 1893. We have done our best to recreate 221b. Welcome. Orientation is about to commence. Follow me." She turned to her left and led them down the hallway to a door at the end. Turning the brass doorknob, she opened the door and marched into a small room that looked like it had once been someone's flat. Cozy couches, armchairs, and end tables furnished the room. "Please find a seat."

The room boasted other boys and girls and a few adults sitting on couches and armchairs. The youngest child looked to be around eight, while the oldest could have been fifteen. One couch remained unoccupied. Auntie Ei herded Rollie and Cecily over to that couch. Just in time too.

A man entered the room and took his place behind a podium—a formal gesture compared to the informal seating arrangements. He wore a brown suit and pink tie, matching the militant woman who guarded the door. He was very tall and thin, topped with a receding hairline. Subtle bags drooped beneath his keen eyes, yet he did not appear tired.

His sharp facial features—hawk-like nose, square chin, and prominent forehead—were strikingly similar to those of the great detective.

"Welcome to Sherlock Academy of Fine Sleuths. I am Headmaster Sullivan P. Yardsly. I am very happy to see you all here. Let's not waste any time, but let's get right down to business. What is the business at hand, you ask? Well…" He presented a white poster from behind the podium. On the poster the Five Ws plus HOW listed down one side: WHO, WHAT, WHERE, WHEN, and WHY.

Rollie elbowed Cecily and she smiled back.

"WHO!" Headmaster Yardsly boomed, causing everyone to jump, especially a plump boy chewing gum. Back at a normal pitch, he continued. "We are searching for students with heightened skills in deductive reasoning with the potential to be great detectives. Today is our second day of orientation, and we have three more to go in hopes of enrolling gifted students in our school. This brings me to our next question:

"WHAT!" Again Headmaster Yardsly made everyone jump. A little girl with golden ringlets clapped her hands over her ears. "As you know, this school is named the Sherlock Academy of Fine Sleuths in honor of the finest sleuth who ever worked in London. This school is sanctioned by the government, but operates independently of it. We seek to train future detectives to follow in the footsteps of our dear Holmes." Here he paused to take a sip of water that he procured from behind the podium.

"WHERE!" Yardsly still caught them off guard. "You are currently sitting in an old flat in the most famous building ever located on Baker Street, or in London, in my opinion. Yes, this is *the* address where Sherlock Holmes and his dear comrade Dr. Watson resided. How can that be, you ask? The government has kindly granted me the rights to restore and remodel the building to use for the academy.

"WHEN! Classes are Monday through Friday nine to four. We provide housing for students here, which you might find convenient. We include basic academia to keep up with standard education, but our main focus is teaching skills to create future detectives." He paused and everyone braced for his next shout.

"WHY! With the rate of crime increasing and the state of Europe growing more uncertain, the government believes we should invest in future crime-fighters. It's hoped a number of our graduates will join Scotland Yard, the Metropolitan Police, or open private investigations." He took another sip.

"HOW! For a reasonable tuition, students will live and study here. They will complete a four-year basic training. What is that basic training called, you ask? We call it *The Sign of the Four*." He chuckled over his reference to Holmes' case. Getting no response to the inside Sherlockian joke, he continued. "After completing the four-year training, students have several options they can choose from. They may choose to return to normal schooling like secondary school or college, or choose to enroll in Scotland Yard's Apprentice Detective Program, or choose to enroll in our upper class training that paves the way for private investigation practices. I hope that answers all your questions." Headmaster Yardsly took a sip and blinked around the room.

Of course that did not answer all their questions, but everybody was too overwhelmed to ask more. Everyone sat very still and stared at the headmaster, except for a grandfatherly man who wrapped his arm around a skinny bug-eyed boy.

"Good. If there are no more questions, I would like to ask all the potential students to please follow Ms. Katherine E. Yardsly—she's my colleague and sister. Please bring your favorite book with you."

Rollie and Cecily bounced up from the couch. Auntie Ei tugged on Rollie's sleeve.

"Rollin, trust your instincts," she said with much seriousness, giving him a curt nod.

Why would she tell him that now? He did not know if he possessed any instincts. Oh well.

Rollie caught up with Cecily at the door and followed the rest of the children down the hallway. There were four other boys and four other girls, making an even ten with himself and Cecily. Was there any significance to this number? Had they all received letters like he had? A further question nagged him: how did this so-called school even know about him, know about his love for detecting and for the great Holmes? He hoped more answers would trickle from Ms. Katherine E. Yardsly.

"Here we are," Ms. Yardsly announced more loudly than necessary. She opened a door off the hallway and led the children inside.

They found themselves in what had once been a small flat. Now it appeared to serve as a library. The walls displayed bookcases touching all the way to the ceiling. A few ladders rested against them, giving access to the tippy-top shelf. One brown leather armchair and adjoining end table with a green banker's lamp stood as the only other furniture, for there was no more room with so many bookcases. The unusual thing about this library was a minor detail, but still worth wondering about: the books on the shelves lay on their sides, stacked atop each other, as opposed to standing on end side by side like other librarys' books.

"Take a good look around, children," Ms. Yardsly commanded, again too loudly. She planted herself in the dead center of the room and spread her arms wide. "Any comments?" She looked from one child to the other.

Rollie raised his hand, unsure how to address her.

"Yes, Rollin E. Wilson?"

"Why do you stack the books vertically instead of lining them up side by side?"

The other children nodded their approval of this question they had wanted to ask, too.

"You'll soon know the reason. Children, now comes the moment of decision. You must decide right now if you want to commit to Sherlock Academy. You will show me your answer with one of two actions. If you wish to attend, simply place your favorite book on the end table. If you do not wish to attend, simply hug your book to yourself."

The children looked around at each other, not quite sure what to decide. What a small gesture for so grand a decision!

A round little boy about Rollie's age asked, "Can I ask my parents first? I don't know what they want me to do."

"No, this is *your* commitment."

"I don't think I'll like this school," the little girl with golden ringlets muttered as she hugged her book and stepped back toward the door.

"Very well. No hard feelings. You made the right decision for yourself," Ms. Yardsly stated very matter-of-factly. "Quickly, children, quickly."

One dark-haired boy whose pants were a bit short stepped forward and slapped his book on the end table. "This is all very mysterious. I like it."

Rollie agreed with this opinion. He really wanted to join in a mystery, but he knew so little about it. Would he like the school? Were his parents in favor of him enrolling? He wished he had more information…but then it would not be a mystery. He felt a flutter in his middle, a good flutter. Nope, if he wanted to be a detective, he must not second-guess his—instincts! *Rollin, trust your instincts,* he heard Auntie Ei's encouraging words in his head.

He placed his beloved Sherlock Holmes volume on top of the other boy's book. He sneaked a glance at the title: *The Hound of the Baskervilles.*

Cecily came up behind him and stacked her book *The Casebook of Sherlock Holmes* on top of his. She stifled a smile. Another girl with little spectacles set down her book *A Study in Scarlet.* Rollie grimaced. His fear that everyone would bring a Sherlock Holmes book proved true...at least for those joining the academy. So far they were the only four. The other six children stood by the door, books pressed close to their chests. Rollie wondered what their titles were. He stepped nearer and read a few of their spines: *Peter Pan, The Wind in the Willows, Alice in Wonderland, The Swiss Family Robinson...*He strained to read the last two. *Peter Pan* again, and...*Aesop's Fables.* No Sherlock Holmes. Hmm...

"Children, you may return to your adults right down the hall," Ms. Yardsly instructed. "Except you four. Stay a moment." She waited until the six had vacated the room, then she scooped up the favorite books on the end table and headed toward a wall of bookshelves. Randomly, she stacked each book in an empty space. Then she spun back around to the children. "Could you find your books again?"

Rollie glanced at Cecily. The other boy and girl regarded each other. They all shrugged. That seemed too easy. They could see their books atop different stacks on the shelves. They all nodded.

"Rollin E. Wilson."

"Yes, madam?"

"You asked why we stack our books instead of lining them up beside each other."

"Yes?"

Without another word, Ms. Yardsly flicked the light switch on. No one had noticed no light fixture on the ceiling. Instantly, an extraordinary thing happened before their eyes. With a whooshing and thumping sound much like wind banging shutters, the bookshelves slid aside or dropped or rose. One shelf divider slid to the right, pushing a stack of books with it. The shelf the stack rested on suddenly gave way like a trap door, plopping the stack of books down to the shelf below it. Another shelf divider slid that stack to the left, making way for the shelf below to rise and propel a new stack of books up through the trap door. The new stack of books rested on the shelf where the first stack of books had previously been.

This was just one example of the dizzying motion. The entire library rearranged as every single bookshelf relocated every single stack of books. So quickly did the library change, the children practically gasped for breath. Ms. Yardsly flicked the light switch off, halting the library.

She turned to the four astounded children and asked, "Now could you find your book?"

They stared at her, then at the bookshelves that were anything but recognizable.

"That will be your ongoing case to solve. You must discover the pattern of the movable shelves and find your book," Ms. Yardsly told them. As she turned to leave, she added, "The library is on its own timer. It rearranges every twenty-four hours."

"So there is a distinct pattern to how they move?" Cecily asked, fascinated.

"Why on earth would you want a library like that?" the dark-haired boy wondered. "You'd never be able to find anything!"

"Yes, you would, if you knew the pattern," Cecily argued.

"If we don't solve this case, we don't get our favorite book back?" the girl with glasses asked, sounding upset. "That's not fair."

"It's a great strategy," Rollie added. "It's one way to make sure you stay committed. You wouldn't drop out, unless you didn't really care about your book."

"Is that true?" the girl asked.

Ms. Yardsly ignored their questions and concerns. She marched down the hallway to the room where the adults waited. When they entered, they were surprised to find only Auntie Ei, a petite dark-haired woman, and Headmaster Sullivan P. Yardsly waiting for them. The headmaster still stood at his podium, facing the two women in their seats. When the children and Ms. Yardsly entered, he shot his hands up in the air.

"Hooray for our new students!" he beamed. "I am so excited to enroll you. Why am I excited, you ask? I believe you are very gifted children. I look forward to training you into fine detectives. What did you think of the Rearranging Library? Cecily A. Brighton?"

"I think it's brilliant!" Cecily exclaimed.

"It's very mysterious," the dark-haired boy muttered.

Headmaster Yardsly pointed a slender, delicate finger at him. "That's the word I sought, Eliot S. Tilden. Anyone else? What did you think, Tabbitha A. Smith?"

"I suppose it's interesting, but I definitely want my book back."

"Rollin E. Wilson?"

"It's very clever. I mean to solve the pattern."

"That's the spirit! Students, take a knee."

The four children were a little taken aback, but after witnessing that whooshing library, nothing seemed too strange now. They knelt down. Headmaster Yardsly reached behind his podium and brought out a stack of four broad boxes. He presented each student with one.

"Welcome to Sherlock Academy, sleuths!"

CHAPTER 4

Shakespeare's Secret

The cab bounced along the road, the driver snapping the reins every so often. Auntie Ei sat stiff and proper, occasionally glancing out a little side window. Rollie sat snugly between her and Cecily. After informing Ms. Yardsly that Cecily lived three doors down from the Wilson manor, Cecily hitched a ride with them. Since the hansom was intended for two passengers, the three of them sat cozily close together. Both Rollie and Cecily balanced broad rectangular boxes on their laps. The boxes resembled board game boxes and were wrapped with brown paper and string. Little tags with strict instructions dangled from the string: *New Student Admissions Package. Do not open until safely home.*

"I wonder if this is anything like the admissions package I got in the mail a few weeks ago," Cecily wondered aloud.

"You got an admissions package from them already?" Rollie asked, his brown eyes showing a little hurt.

"No, not from them. It's from the all-girls boarding school Mum is thinking of sending me to. Remember? Let's hope she changes her mind and lets me go to this school. This one is much more exciting."

"What was in that admissions package?"

"Forms and forms and more forms. All boring. Just paperwork that had too much print." Cecily rolled her eyes and stuck out her tongue.

Rollie shrugged. "I'll bet this one just has forms and papers for our parents." He rested his hand on his box.

Auntie Ei glanced at them, then back at the window. "Hardly, my dear boy. Hardly."

Rollie studied her and thought he spied a smile play on the corners of her mouth. "Do you know what's in here, Auntie?"

"Rollin, how would I possibly know what is in that box?"

A good question. This school and everything involved with it seemed so mysterious; he could not fathom how anyone could know a thing about it. Yet there were deliberate looks she gave and odd things she said that made Rollie wonder if Auntie Ei knew more than she appeared to.

"Auntie, do you think Mum and Dad will let me go to this school?"

"They'll have to. You need to get your book back."

"They might not think that's a good enough reason."

"Rollin, do you want to attend?"

Rollie nodded eagerly.

"Did you trust your instincts to enroll?"

Rollie nodded again.

Auntie Ei nodded curtly. "Well then, it's settled. Leave your parents to me."

The driver pulled up the reins and hopped down. He opened the doors. "'Ere we are, miss. Number 19 Primrose Lane." He tipped his bowler hat and helped Cecily out of the hansom.

"Bye, Rollie! I'll be over tomorrow." Cecily waved and skipped down her front walkway.

With a flick of the reins, the driver guided the horse three houses down, and stopped. "Number 22 Primrose Lane." He escorted Auntie Ei out. "Good afternoon, Lady Wilson, lad."

Auntie Ei marched up the hedge-lined walkway and through the front double doors. Rollie scampered after her, clutching his box under his arm. They entered just as the grandfather clock in the parlor struck noon. Rollie thought it was later than that, for he felt like he had been gone all day.

They barely took their coats off when Mr. Wilson barged through the front door. During the summer, he finished teaching his courses by late noon and made a point to be home for lunch. He hung his briefcase and fedora on the hall tree and dabbed his brow with his handkerchief.

"Fact: it's a bit warm today. I hope Cook has some fresh lemonade. Oh, Auntie Ei, Rollie, how was your morning at, uh, what's the name of it again?"

Auntie Ei grunted, "Sherlock Academy."

"Dad, they have this library that—"

"Rest easy, son. Let's get some lunch, then you can tell Mum and I all about it." Mr. Wilson led them through the house to the back porch where lunch waited.

"Rollie! Auntie Ei! You're back just in time," Mrs. Wilson exclaimed, kissing Rollie's forehead. "Lunch is ready. I set places for you, hoping you'd be home for lunch."

The family, minus Edward and Stewart who ate their lunch at the shop, scooted around the small table laden with cold meat sandwiches and lemonade. Lucille and Daphne tried to engage the conversation by recounting their mother-daughter tea that morning, but Auntie Ei would not allow it.

"For goodness' sake, you two, stop giggling over your ridiculous tea," the old woman snapped. "The conversation today will be about Rollin and his new school. Rollin, do you have the admissions package?"

Rollie reached down beside his chair and hoisted up the box. "Should I open it?"

"You are safely home, are you not? Open it!"

Rollie slipped off the string, then peeled off the paper, slowly at first, then more feverishly, the way he opened presents. A box, as he had guessed. A long envelope addressed to his parents rested atop the lid. He handed it to his father.

Mr. Wilson pushed his spectacles farther up his nose and ripped open the envelope. He slipped out a folded piece of paper and flapped it open. He cleared his throat, but read it silently. His brow furrowed with every line he read.

"What does it say, Peter?" Mrs. Wilson asked. "Read it aloud." To herself she muttered, "I don't understand why these Wilson men must keep everything a secret."

"It's all very..." he stammered, searching for the right word.

"Mysterious?" Rollie ventured.

"Yes, exactly, son. Mysterious."

Rollie beamed. He hoped for just that when he opened the package.

Mr. Wilson cleared his throat again and read:

"To the Parents of Rollin E. Wilson,

It gives us great pleasure to admit your talented son to our esteemed academy. We have no doubt he will thrive here and be an asset to our staff and students, as well as to all of England someday.

Rollin E. Wilson has been specially selected from students all over the United Kingdom to enroll in our program that will enhance and utilize his fine abilities in deductive reasoning, spatial awareness, and high IQ. We ask only for your willingness to share him and his willingness to attend.

Below you will find the who, what, where, when, why, and how discussed earlier today. That should answer any additional questions you may have. Classes begin 1 August—we take short summer holidays! Rollin has the option of boarding at our school or commuting during the week. That decision is entirely up to you and him. Either way, an anonymous benefactor will pay for his tuition.

Enclosed in the box you will find Rollin's class schedule. He must know his class schedule the first day of school.

With all due respect and gratitude,

Headmaster Sullivan P. Yardsly

Sherlock Academy of Fine Sleuths"

Mr. Wilson took off his spectacles and chewed on one of the ends. "There you have it. The fact still remains that this is all very...mysterious."

"I don't quite understand," Mrs. Wilson spoke up. "Would Rollie attend this school in place of or in addition to his regular schooling?"

"In place of," Auntie Ei said. "Headmaster Yardsly explained that they carry on regular instruction in mathematics and language and such. But they also instruct them in detective skills."

"It's like an apprenticeship for an occupation," Mr. Wilson added. "Is it for Scotland Yard?"

"A bit," Auntie Ei agreed, biting a cold salmon sandwich.

"Rollie, is this something you want to do?" Mr. Wilson asked seriously.

"Yes, Dad, I really want to."

"Eloise?"

"Can it be trusted as a school of quality education?" Mrs. Wilson asked doubtfully.

"Absolutely!" Auntie Ei exclaimed in a tone of offense.

Rollie held his breath, itching to hear his parents' consent and itching to open the box on his lap. He observed his parents communicate with their eyes, as they often did before declaring a decision aloud.

"Very well, son, open the box," his father shrugged again.

Rollie gripped the edges and slowly pulled up the lid. He stared a moment, again taken aback. A large, very thick, hardback leather-bound book lay in the box. "*The Complete Works of William Shakespeare,*" he deadpanned, almost too low to be heard. If he had not been so mystified, he may have groaned aloud in disappointment. He hoped a class schedule or spy gadgets were in the box. He loved books, but he had plenty of those. The family library housed all Shakespeare's works.

"Rollin, do not judge a book by its cover," Auntie Ei told him sternly. "Open the book."

He opened the cover. A deep hole had been carved through the pages of the book. In that hole lay five random items. One by one, Rollie showed them to his family:

One large skeleton key with 0900A engraved on its stem.

One smoking pipe (resembling what Holmes would smoke) with 1130F inscribed on the side.

One ballpoint pen with 1300H typed on the cap.

One small vial of what appeared to be dust labeled with 1030D.

One red felt ball cap embroidered with 1400G on the brim.

"All of that was in the book?" Mrs. Wilson asked, surprised.

"It's a hollow book, Mum. See?" Rollie held up the book to show her the cavity carved into it. He noticed the inside cover marked *Personal Property of Rollin E. Wilson.* "It's a great way to keep your stuff secret because everybody thinks it's a book."

"Fact: that's an ingenious method for keeping your property private," Mr. Wilson stated, a twinkle of excitement in his brown eyes. "I might employ the same method for my own secrets."

"What secrets do you have, dearest?" Mrs. Wilson asked, a little alarmed.

"Oh you know, birthday gifts for my wife, or the combination to our safe."

"I think you might invent some secrets so you can have a hollow book to keep them in."

"Perhaps, Eloise."

"Rollin, read us your class schedule," Auntie Ei cut in, picking out onions from her sandwich.

Rollie's brow furrowed as he searched the inside of the book. "There is no class schedule."

"But the letter said the class schedule was enclosed," Auntie Ei insisted.

"Nothing in here but those objects." Rollie tipped the book upside-down, hoping an explanation would fall from it.

"It certainly is mysterious." Mrs. Wilson poured Lucille more lemonade. "Perhaps a little too mysterious for comfort."

Auntie Ei shook her head. "That's the way it must be. It does little good to merely *teach* students how to solve mysteries. They must *apply* their skills to realistic situations. I guarantee that this class schedule is just the beginning of all the mysteries Rollin will have to solve to get through a day at school. It's good for him."

Rollie stared at the mysterious items on the table. *Enclosed you will find Rollin's class schedule.* Were these items related to his classes? What did these numbers and letters on each item signify? That flutter of excitement grew in his middle as the mystery grew in his mind.

CHAPTER 5

Timetables and Such

"*I* have never been more relieved in all my life," Cecily exclaimed.

In the third floor bedroom, she and Rollie sat at his desk under the window. They took turns peeping through the telescope, then through the binoculars. They watched Mr. Crenshaw in his garden below. The elderly gentleman lounged in his favorite chair under a willow tree, sorting through his briefcase. The angle was just right, allowing the two little sleuths to read the papers he shuffled through. Periodically he sipped his coffee.

"I mean, just a few weeks ago I was worried about going to this all-girls boarding school in Newcastle," Cecily continued. "Newcastle! That's way up north. Now I'm going to this brilliant school where I get to do what I like best. I get to go with my best friend, too. How did my luck change?"

"Actually, I have no idea," Rollie commented. "I was sure your mum wouldn't let you go. What made her say 'yes'?"

Cecily focused the binoculars. "A few things. First, I can board there. Also the tuition is *way* more inexpensive than the Newcastle school. And I begged a lot."

"How much is the tuition?" Rollie watched Mr. Crenshaw ring a little bell. In response, his young brassy-haired secretary emerged from the house, a notepad and pen in her hands, her high-heels *clippety-clopping* across the patio.

"Didn't you read your letter?"

"Someone is paying for my tuition."

"Who?"

"I don't know. An anonymous benefactor."

Cecily looked at him. "That's interesting. Sure it's not your family?"

"They couldn't be anonymous…even if they tried. My family can't keep anything a secret."

"Good point. Who else knows about you and the school?"

"I have no idea," Rollie shrugged.

"Well, that's great—about your tuition."

"I know, but it makes me wonder."

"You know what I wonder about, Rollie?"

"What?"

"I still wonder how we got chosen. How did the school know about our skills and all that?"

"Do you think Mrs. Simmons had something to do with it?" Rollie wondered.

He thought a lot about his past teacher. One day in April she had caught him making notes in his journal about Anthony Greene, who he suspected of stealing the class candy jar. It was a big mystery for about a week. Rollie had been afraid that Mrs. Simmons would punish him, but instead she encouraged him to pursue solving the case, just not during math. After that she had several conversations with him about his love for Sherlock Holmes and his love for solving mysteries. Rollie had mentioned that Cecily also enjoyed the same hobby. On the last day of final exams, Mrs. Simmons had added one more exam, not typically given to ten year old students. The exam contained ten unusual and complicated questions. Although Rollie had felt good about his answers, he never saw the results.

"I was thinking the same thing!" Cecily gasped. "Remember that exam? So weird. What were some of the questions?"

"*If you are looking at a rainbow, where is the sun located?*" Rollie cited. "There was something about a chess position too."

"Oh! And there were a bunch of questions where you had to predict the pattern or something."

"I wonder if that was a test to find students with certain skills. Like what the academy was looking for."

"That makes a lot of sense. I wonder if every teacher gave that exam, or just Mrs. Simmons."

"I don't know, but Mr. Crenshaw has his bank statement out." Rollie squinted through the telescope. "Ready? Current balance 12,412 pounds."

"He's so wealthy." In her little notepad, Cecily jotted down the amount underneath a long list of amounts. "Wait a minute. He made a large purchase since last week."

"He went to London that one day, remember? When we shared our letters."

"What did he buy?"

"He's going through his receipts now," Rollie said. "The post office….a bookstore…a pub…a florist…"

"Oo, a florist. Who did he send flowers to?"

Rollie shrugged. "The city clerk."

"He sent flowers to the city clerk?"

"No, he has a receipt from the city clerk."

"Oh. How much?"

"His thumb is in the way…I think it says 150 pounds."

"Whoa, that's a large purchase. What did he purchase exactly?" Cecily quizzed.

"I don't know, his fingers are in the way. Don't you think it's funny that he always wears gloves? Even in the summer?" Rollie focused the binoculars.

"Sort of, although I know gentlemen are fond of wearing gloves."

"But usually when they go out. Not in their own garden."

"Maybe something's wrong with his hands."

Rollie nodded. "Maybe. Come to think of it, I've never seen his hands without them."

"I guess that's just one of his idiotcrisies," Cecily shrugged.

"His what?"

"You know, a funny thing that makes someone unique. Isn't it idisuncrisies or something like that?"

"You mean id-i-o-syn-cra-sies," Rollie pronounced with a chuckle.

"That's what I said."

"Wait—another invoice." Rolling pressed his right eye to the telescope. "Paid to M.U.S."

"Not those mysterious initials again! They pop up everywhere."

"I wish we knew what they stood for."

"I'm sick of not knowing what they mean."

"Drat, he's going inside." Rollie watched Mr. Crenshaw stand up from his chair, stretch a bit, and take his brief case into the large house. His secretary followed. "That's probably all for today."

"What do you want to work on now?"

"How about our *class schedule*," Rollie intonated these last words with sarcasm. He loved mysteries, but hated ones that stumped him too long. A week had passed, and still those items in the hollow book baffled him.

Cecily sighed. "I did figure one thing out."

"You did?"

"We have the same class schedule."

Rollie socked her gently in the shoulder. "Ha, ha. Elementary, my dear Watson."

"Let's think about this. What information is on a normal class schedule?"

Rollie grabbed his notepad and pencil stub. "Time of the class. Name of the class. Name of the professor teaching the class. The room the class is in. That's what are on those college class schedules my dad has. Have you come up with anything?"

"Maybe the item has something to do with the class."

"I thought of that too." Rollie flipped through his notepad to a list. "The cap could represent P.E."

"Good one. The pen could be Grammar. What about that vial of dust?"

"Science? You know how we studied weird things under a microscope. What about the pipe?"

"That one has me stumped," Cecily admitted. "And the key."

"We don't have anything for math or history."

"History is the key to the present?"

"A far stretch. How about math is the key to…" Rollie trailed off, feeling a bit defeated. "I think we're off. This seems too iffy."

Cecily nodded in agreement. "Any student could interpret these objects any way. There's got to be something more concrete."

Rollie picked up the key and studied it. "These numbers and letters are concrete."

"Let's study those." Cecily turned the pipe over in her hands.

"These numbers and letters could be the course ID," Rollie suggested.

"What do you mean?"

"College courses have titles and numbers and letters. My dad teaches math course number 102A and 102B."

"That makes sense! So this class is course number 1130F. It has something to do with pipes? If that's the case, then we can't do anything more until we go to school and look up their class courses. How can we know what class is 1130F?"

Rollie frowned. It made sense, but he expected a little more from this mystery. He remembered the academy expected him to arrive the first day of school and know his class schedule. Was he missing something else? Were his detecting skills not as fine as he had come to believe? Maybe he was not qualified for Sherlock Academy.

"I don't think that's it either," he finally conceded.

"I think that's it," Cecily countered. She stood up and stretched. "Until we go, we can't know anything more. I need a snack."

Rollie followed her out of the bedroom and down the two flights of stairs. They found their way to the spacious kitchen where Cook was boiling lobsters on the stove.

"Hello, Cook, we need a snack," Rollie announced.

"Do you now? It's nearly four and dinner's at six, so don't be eatin' nothin' too hearty, d'ya hear?"

"We won't. How about an apple? We can split it." Rollie reached up to the hanging basket and selected a pippin apple. He carefully cut it down the middle with a knife and handed one half to Cecily. "The garden?"

Cecily bit into her half and nodded. The two scampered out the kitchen and onto the back patio. They leaned against the mulberry tree, eating their halves. At first they heard only the chomp-munch, chomp-munch of their apple eating. Soon they were joined by voices on the other side of the tall brick wall. They recognized Mr. Crenshaw and his secretary whose name they could never overhear.

"Sir, I have the time table here. Did you wish to depart at eleven-thirty or twelve-fifteen?"

"Eleven-thirty would be best. Cable Herr Zhimmer and request his chauffeur to meet me at the depot when I arrive."

"Very good, sir. Will you be needing anything else?"

"No, I fancy a bit of reading now."

Clip-clop, her heels receded into the house. They heard a contented sigh, and no more.

Cecily shrugged and chomped away. Rollie chewed thoughtfully on his bite, slowly at first, then quicker as an idea shed light in his mind.

"That makes sense!" he suddenly exclaimed, leaping to his feet.

"Shh! He's still outside," Cecily cautioned, pointing to the brick wall.

"No, not *him*. The class schedule!"

"I thought we already made sense of that."

Rollie raced into the house, Cecily close at his heels. He bounded up the stairs, two at a time, clinging to the banister for support. He flew into his bedroom and dropped to his knees. He picked up the closest object, the vial of dust, and read the numbers.

"One, zero, three, zero."

"Yeah, so?"

"Or you could say ten-thirty."

"Sure."

"Don't you see? This is the time. Just like the train timetable that the secretary mentioned to Mr. Crenshaw. On a timetable the numbers are written just like this one, with no break. But you know it's a time so you say eleven-thirty. Or *ten-thirty*!" Rollie passed the vial of dust to Cecily.

Cecily's eyes sparkled. "I think you're on to something. That makes more sense. You said class schedules had the times on them."

Rollie studied the pipe. "This class starts at eleven-thirty. See?"

"Okay, what about the key?" She passed him the key with a doubtful expression.

The numbers on the key were 0900. Rollie studied it a moment, and brightened. "Nine o'clock. The timetables put a zero first if it's a single-digit hour."

"Good. Oh, hold it, Holmes, the pen and the cap throw everything off. The pen is 1300 and—"

"And the cap is 1400. Gees, I thought I was on to something." His shoulders slumped a bit.

Cecily laid out the pipe, the vial of dust, and the key on the floor in a row, and rearranged them.

"What are you doing?" Rollie wondered.

"Putting the times in order. Nine o'clock first, then ten-thirty, then eleven-thirty."

"I don't think they're times. The pen and cap don't make sense."

"Let's just say they are times and this is part of the schedule," Cecily continued. "We have a class at nine, then let's say we have morning recess. Remember at our old school we had a morning recess around ten. Next class, ten-thirty. Next class eleven-thirty. If they're hour long classes, we'd get out at twelve-thirty."

"Then probably lunch," Rollie added.

"Which would be an hour. Our next class would have to be at one o'clock at least."

"Then a class at 1300 and 1400? There's no such—wait! Yes, there is! In military time, 1300 *is* one o'clock!"

"You're right!" Cecily squealed. "So 1400 would be two o'clock?"

"Yes! We did it! We've got our class schedule!" Rollie slapped a high-five with Cecily. "That makes more sense than course numbers."

"But we still have these letters," she reminded him.

Both of them returned to hunched postures and furrowed brows.

Cecily spoke up first, breaking the silence of concentration. "Maybe the letters are course ID's."

"They could, but again that doesn't help us till we get to school," Rollie objected. "We're supposed to figure out the class schedule before we go."

"What else could these letters mean then? What information are we missing?"

"Professor's name, course name, and location."

Sucking on the tip of his pencil, Rollie thought. One letter, not a few letters, so they could not be initials. What could just one letter represent? A lock combination? He thought of things involving one letter. A grid, a set of building directions like what his model planes came with, an address, a—

"Flats!" he shouted.

"What?"

"The letter is the address of a flat! Like 221 *b*!"

"The school *is* an apartment building!"

"I bet the flats are the classrooms. So that class—whatever it is—probably is in flat H at 221!"

"Well, done, Holmes!"

"Why thank you." Rollie grinned and bowed dramatically.

"Now we're getting somewhere. We know the times and places."

"I still want to know what the class is, or who is teaching it."

"Should we go back to our first guess?" Cecily ventured, holding up the ballpoint pen. "Grammar?"

Rollie shrugged. "That could be true, but what about these other items? What class would need a pipe or a key?"

"Who knows? Remember, this school is very out of the ordinary. I wouldn't rule out any possibility."

"That should be our new motto: *don't rule out any possibility.*"

"I like it. We should wear badges that say it."

"Let's review our class schedule, shall we?" Rollie said in his professor impersonation. Whenever he wanted to sound important, he thickened his British accent and deepened his voice to impersonate his father, whom he thought was the epitome of a professor. This always made Cecily giggle.

He cleared his throat. "Fact: young lady, at nine o'clock you have a class in room A. From there you have recess, I'm assuming. Fact: you attend a class having to do with vials of dust at ten-thirty in room D." Here he paused and held up the vial and shook it a bit. "Next you must go to room F at eleven-thirty where you will learn to smoke a pipe. Not very lady-like, but I guess that won't bother you."

Cecily rolled with laughter. "Stop it! Let's write this down on paper."

"What, my silly impersonation?"

"No, twit, this class schedule." Cecily regained her composure and scribbled down the class schedule as follows:

Key	9:00am	Room A
Recess	10:00am	?
Vial	10:30am	Room D
Pipe	11:30am	Room F
Lunch	12:30pm	?
Pen	1:00pm	Room H
Cap	2:00pm	Room G

"Looks great," Rollie commented, glancing at the schedule over her shoulder.

"School is out at three? I thought they said classes went till four."

"Maybe till four there are special activities that change every day, like music and PE and drama. Like at our old school."

"Maybe. Just when I think we've got it, something else pops up mysterious!"

Rollie grinned. "Do you think there's information in those words? I hadn't thought about it till you wrote them out. Key, recess, vial, pipe…"

"I hadn't thought of it either. Maybe. Like a code?"

Rollie did not answer, but studied the words. He read them backwards. Key became yek. Yuck, that did not work. He inserted the room letter A into the word. He came up with akey, kaey, keay, keya…that was too unnerving. He rearranged the letters in key: eky, eyk, yek, yke….nothing sounded remotely like a course or a professor's name.

A little light flickered through his brain.

"Initials?" he and Cecily both chimed at the same time.

"Rollie, your initials are REW. Mine are CAB. See? Mine spell a word."

"I wish mine spelled a word," Rollie muttered.

"Sorry about that. These words could be the initials of our teachers."

"We don't know any of their names. We only met the headmaster and his sister."

"Once we get to school and look at the directory, we'll know right away."

"The sister!" Rollie gasped. "What was her name? Katherine something Yardsly?"

"I can't remember her middle initial, but I'm willing to bet my left over chocolate Easter bunny that her middle initial is E."

"You still have your Easter bunny? It's July!"

Cecily shrugged. "Beside the point. We have a class with KEY: Katherine E. Yardsly. We solved the mystery of the class schedule. I'm exhausted." She fell back dramatically onto the floor, her eyes closed and her arms sprawled out.

CHAPTER 6

August the First

$\mathcal{H}$aving solved the class schedule, Rollie felt more confident and thrilled about attending Sherlock Academy—until he realized that two of the words, VIAL and PIPE, had four letters. He rethought his idea about the initials. He mentioned this to Cecily the next day, and she assured him that some people had *two* middle names or, in some rare cases, *two* last names. They decided to count this as a possibility and stick to their theory.

Much to their surprise, the days trickled by quickly, and before they knew it, the end of July came. On Sunday, the day before August first, the Wilson household erupted into chaos in preparation for Rollie's first day of school. Lucille and Daphne pointed out they were luckier than him because their summer holiday continued until September. Edward and Stewart warned everyone they were not taking Rollie to school every day, until Mr. Wilson reminded them that Rollie would be boarding there and would be brought home every Friday evening for the weekend by the academy's taxi service. Mrs. Wilson asked Rollie if he remembered to pack his toothbrush, and his slippers, and his bathrobe, and "oh, what about your nice slacks, and don't forget a copy of the family portrait". Auntie Ei remained the only calm person in the manor that afternoon. She sat in the library, appearing to read, but really eavesdropping on everyone.

As Rollie passed the open library door, she *psst!* at him. "Rollin, come in here a moment."

Rollie hurried into the library. "What is it, Auntie? Mother wants me to grab my—"

"Never mind about that right now. I have something important to give you." She reached under her armchair and held out an ordinary looking jar of marmalade. "Take it."

Rollie took it, confused. It was a small jar, holding maybe one cup of orange marmalade. It was sealed with wax, and labeled with a tag that read *A good snack for the LIBRARY*. "Uh, thanks, Auntie."

"You're very welcome, Rollin. Perhaps it will remind you of home."

"Perhaps." As far as he could remember, no one ate marmalade on toast in the Wilson house. He was not about to hurt the old woman's feelings, so he nodded in agreement.

"When you've eaten it all, save the jar. You may find it useful."

"Okay."

"Now run along and finish packing." Auntie Ei returned her attention to her book.

As Rollie left the library, she called after him, "Don't forget to pack that marmalade!"

*   *   *   *

The next morning, being the first of August and thus the first day of school for Rollie, the Wilson household grew more chaotic than the previous night. The whole family crowded together in the entry hall, along with Rollie's one suitcase and two boxes. Rollie endured farewell pinches and hair ruffling from his older twin brothers, and dainty hugs from his younger twin sisters. When the horse-drawn hansom pulled up to the house on time, the family pressed together for a final farewell.

"Wash behind your ears, and air your socks and—"

"Eloise, that's enough," Mr. Wilson cut in. "Rollie's a good boy. He'll be fine."

"He's never gone away to school before. Not even to camp."

"Mum, I'll be home on the weekends."

"Or sooner," Edward smirked. "Stew and I have a bet that you'll get homesick by Wednesday."

"I'm saying Thursday," Stewart added. "He'll be home by Thursday."

"Son, I'm saying Friday."

"Dad, that's the plan, to come home on Fridays."

"I know, son, I'm joking with you." Mr. Wilson gave him a wink and a firm squeeze on the shoulder. "Time to go." He picked up Rollie's suitcase and carried it to the cab. "Boys, grab his boxes!"

Grumbling, the twins each picked up a box and carried it to the cab. Lucille and Daphne helped each other carry his book bag. Mrs. Wilson pulled Rollie to her and hugged him.

"Be safe, and be good," she whispered in his ear. "Study hard and have fun."

"Bye, Mum. I'll see you in a week." Rollie turned to Auntie Ei. He leaned in for a hug, and she patted his back.

"Do you have that jar of marmalade?"

"Yes, Auntie, in one of those boxes."

"Good boy. Keep your eyes and ears open and trust your instincts." She nodded curtly and gave him a nudge down the front steps.

As Rollie neared the front gate, he gaped in astonishment at who was there to meet him.

"Good morning, Mr. Crenshaw!" Mr. Wilson called.

At a closer distance, Rollie noticed the neighbor's firm jaw and fine wrinkles around his eyes. Mr. Crenshaw tipped his hat, and held out a thick parchment envelope in his gloved hand.

"Would you do me the service of delivering this letter to a Professor Ichabod P. Enches?" Mr. Crenshaw asked gravely. "He is an old friend of mine and I have wanted to contact him."

With some shock, Rollie took the large envelope and nodded. "Where can I find him?"

"At the school you are attending. You will find him or he will find you. Thank you ever so much." He tipped his hat again, turned, and strolled down the sidewalk back to his mansion.

Letter in hand, Rollie watched the old neighbor leave. His mind started asking questions, but the cab driver urged him to go. Rollie waved to his family as he climbed inside. The driver flicked the reins and started the hansom down the road. Rollie studied the sealed envelope. He read the name printed on the front: *Professor Ichabod P. Enches.* Such an odd name, but Rollie had learned long ago not to judge someone's name since his was also unusual. As he studied the name, the letters popped up from the page at him.

"PIPE!" he exclaimed to himself. "I can't wait to tell Cecily!"

On the back of the envelope, he noticed those strange initials molded from the sealing wax: M.U.S. Soon the hansom stopped at Cecily's house. She waited alone by the front gate. As the driver loaded her luggage, she climbed inside.

"Where's your family?" Rollie asked. "Didn't they want to say goodbye?"

"I said goodbye to them this morning," Cecily shrugged. "Did you have a whole farewell procession?"

"Guess what? I know who PIPE stands for."

"Who?"

Rollie held up the letter and watched her read it, then brighten.

"Where did you get that?"

"You'll never guess. Mr. Crenshaw gave it to me to give to this professor at our school."

"That's very strange."

"I know! We learned another teacher's name out of it. I can't wait to get there!" He practically bounced on his seat in anticipation.

The anticipation lasted another twenty minutes until they stopped at 221 Baker Street. The driver jumped down from his perch and opened the cab doors. "Go 'head and check in. I'll deliver yer luggage to yer rooms."

As they hopped out of the cab, Rollie and Cecily noticed the street crowded with hansoms and a long line of children leading to the front door. They found the end of the line at the corner of the building and stepped into place.

"I didn't know this many students went here," Rollie commented.

"Me either. When we came to that orientation, there weren't this many," Cecily agreed.

A short blond boy turned around and said, "A lot of us are *returning* students. Only a few are *new* students." He turned back around and said no more to them.

In the distance, Big Ben announced the time of eight-thirty. At that moment, the line moved forward as the front doors opened. When Rollie and Cecily reached the front doors, they found a welcome sign that instructed them to find their first class of the day.

"This is it," Rollie exhaled. "This is when we find out if we solved the class schedule." He pulled out his notepad from his inner coat pocket and flipped to the schedule he and Cecily had jotted down. "Room A should be on this ground floor." He led Cecily down a hallway with other children.

The only rooms on the first floor were the headmaster's office, the library, the orientation room, and a locked storage closet. They ventured upstairs to the second floor and quickly found room A. The one-time flat had been converted into a classroom with individual desks and chairs facing a blackboard. Several charts covered the walls. The charts did not make sense, all having to do with numbers and letters arranged oddly. Unsure if there was a seating chart, Rollie and Cecily chose two desks side-by-side two rows from the front.

"I like to be close," Cecily whispered.

"But not too close in case we're wrong and have to leave," Rollie added, sliding into his chair.

As the clock ticked towards nine o'clock, several students filed into the classroom, all wearing similar expressions of uncertainty. They chose seats and roved their eyes around. At nine o'clock, the teacher marched into the room and towered in front of the blackboard.

"Welcome to your first class at Sherlock Academy. I am Katherine E. Yardsly."

Nine O'clock

Rollie and Cecily glanced at each other excitedly. So far they were right about the class schedule.

"Students, if you are in the correct class, I will call your name from my roll sheet," Katherine E. Yardsly called, whipping out a sheet of paper from her desk. "If you are not in the correct class, you will return to the entry hall and attempt to solve the class schedule again. Understand?" She looked around the room, but did not seem to want an answer. She snapped her eyes back to the roll sheet. "Brighton!"

"Here!" Cecily answered, and blew a sigh of relief.

"Fraser!"

"Yes, that's me! I'm here!" one pale boy answered, wiping beads of sweat from his forehead.

"Hawkins!"

"Thank goodness!" one dark-haired girl exhaled.

Ms. Yardsly worked down the list, responded by relieved boys and girls. When the name Tildon was called, Rollie recognized him as the dark-haired boy he had met in the rearranging library. Rollie studied him so closely, he jumped when his name was called.

"Wilson!"

"Present!"

"That concludes the class list." She eyed two girls sitting in the back. "Go back downstairs to the foyer and solve the class schedule."

The two girls shyly fumbled to their feet and ducked out the door.

"Good job to you who found your first class, but you still have four other classes. Are there any questions before we commence?"

Cecily raised her hand. "Our class schedule ends with two o'clock, but we were told school goes till four. Where do we go after the two o'clock class?"

"Good observation, Cecily A. Brighton. You will be given more information on that later. Are there any other questions? Good. Let's begin."

Ms. Yardsly turned to the blackboard, grabbed a piece of chalk, and feverishly scribbled on it. Then she spun back around, and stepped aside so the class could read the board. They were not surprised to find that it made no sense.

"Your first assignment is to learn which class this is by decoding what I have written on the board. Use your own ingenuity. You may use the paper and pencil in your desk. You have two minutes. Go!"

Finding just that in his desk, Rollie copied down the letters.

ADBECCDOEDFIGNHG ICJOKULRMSNE OLPEQVRESL TOUNVEW

Rollie focused on the board, his eyes widening, and narrowing. He circled every third letter, like he and Cecily often did when deciphering their own codes. He ended up with BCEI—not a word, so he tried something else. He worked backwards and got VOSVP—not a word either. Time ticked by; a minute left. He squinted again. He circled every other letter and found that every other letter was the alphabet: ABCDEF....The remaining letters spelled...DECODIN—

"Times up! Pencils down! Who has it?"

Eliot S. Tildon shot up his hand. "Decoding Course Level One!"

"You are correct. Sleuths, raise your hands if you cracked the code."

Every hand shot up.

"In this class, you will learn about codes and ciphers. You will learn how to crack the easiest and some of the hardest codes known.

Having a resource of codes and ciphers is invaluable to a detective. You will remember that Sherlock Holmes had on occasion to crack codes. The cipher you cracked here…" Ms. Yardsly tapped the board with her chalk. "…Is one of the simpler ciphers used. You had to circle every other letter to find the message. Second assignment: write down three words to describe me, using this code. You have two minutes. Go!"

Three words to describe her? Rollie thought of three words: icy, stern, and tall. He penciled down these three words, hiding them in the alphabet. He barely finished jotting down the last letter in *tall* when she barked, "Times up, pencils down!"

Every student dropped his pencil and stared up at her. One young girl wearing spectacles, who Rollie remembered from orientation, even put her hands up in the air to show she had dropped her pencil.

"I do a little thing called 'pair-and-share'. You pair up with a partner and share what you've learned. Wherever you have chosen to sit will be your seat the rest of the year. And whomever I assign as your partner today will be your pair-and-share partner for the rest of the term. Understand?" She did not wait for a reply. Instead she maneuvered around the room, pointing to different students, saying, "You and you, partners. You and you, partners…"

Rollie and Cecily were dismayed when Ms. Yardsly did not pair them up. Rollie got paired with Eliot behind him and Cecily got paired with the girl wearing spectacles, whose name, they learned, was Tabbitha—Tibby for short.

"Hey, I remember you from orientation," Eliot said when Rollie turned around in his chair.

"I'm Rollin, but Rollie is fine."

"Eliot, and that's it. I'm not sure there's a way to short-cut Eliot."

"Eli?"

Eliot made a face. "Nope, Eliot it is. How old are you?"

"I'll be eleven on November 1."

"That's still a long ways off. You should just say ten and a half until it's at least October."

Rollie was unsure how seriously to take Eliot, but Eliot seemed to take himself very seriously. "How old are you?"

"I just turned eleven in June."

"That's a while ago."

"Not really. It's a summer birthday and we're still in summer. See, the way I figure it, if your birthday is in the same season as you currently are, then you can say 'I'll be eleven in November.' But if your birthday is in a different season than the current one, then you should just say your age." He nodded firmly, signifying the discussion over.

"I've never heard of that before," Rollie countered. "I think everyone should be able to say what they want. There shouldn't be any rules for that sort of thing."

"If there were more rules, there'd be less crime."

"Maybe, but what do birthdays have to do with crime?"

"Nothing. Rules do."

"I thought we were talking about birthdays."

"You changed the subject," Eliot pointed out.

"No, I didn't, you just said—"

"Rollin E. Wilson!"

Both Rollie and Eliot jumped in their seats. Ms. Yardsly towered over them, her mouth set in a firm line and her eyes locking theirs.

"Let me clarify that pair-and-share time is to be used for assignments, not for your personal banter. Do you understand?"

This time Rollie was sure she wanted an answer. "Yes, Ms. Yardsly."

She held his gaze a moment longer, then ordered, "Swap papers, decode each other's three adjectives, and swap back." She turned on her heel and marched back to the front of the classroom.

Cecily gave Rollie a sympathetic smile, and went back to decoding Tibby's paper. Eliot held out his paper to Rollie. Rollie snatched the paper, tossed his to Eliot, and spun back around in his chair. He quickly circled every other letter and decoded Eliot's three descriptive words: *tall, loud, icy.* Funny that Eliot would use the word *icy* also. Rollie thought it was a creative adjective to use. He turned back around, swapped papers, and returned facing forward.

"Psst!" he heard behind him. "Rollie."

Rollie turned his head a bit. "I'm not talking to you. You got me in trouble."

"Sorry about that, but you should have just agreed with me. Accept my apology, chum?"

Rollie nodded reluctantly.

"Do you get what I'm saying about the birthdays?"

Rollie rolled his eyes. He could not believe Eliot brought it up again, just after they had been warned not to talk. Maybe if he ignored Eliot, then Eliot would get the hint.

"Do you? I think the season really makes a difference. And by the way, do—"

"I don't think this is important," Rollie stressed as he spun around. "So stop talking to me or we'll—"

"Rollin E. Wilson! Did I not just clarify my rules for pair-and-share? Furthermore, pair-and-share is over, so there is no excuse for your turning in your seat and talking with Eliot S. Tildon! You will write the sentence of my choosing one hundred times after class."

Rollie dropped his head on his desk partly in frustration and partly in shame. He waited for Eliot to step up and admit he had contributed to the conversation. No word came from behind. Ms. Yardsly lectured on the history of a few codes, but Rollie barely heard her. He was fuming inside. He was mad at Eliot, but also at himself. He always strove to follow the rules and apply himself as a student. His teachers always liked him and felt proud of him. Now he had made a horrible first impression to his first teacher on the first day of school. He wondered if he should mention Eliot's involvement. No, he did not want to worsen his first impression by being a tattle-tail.

Soon Ms. Yardsly dismissed the class and declared recess for thirty minutes on the rooftop. As the students filed out of the room, she stationed herself behind her desk.

"Rollin E. Wilson, come forth."

Rollie tiptoed up to her desk. He kept his eyes to the floor.

"Take this pencil and paper and write the sentence I dictate to you." She cleared her throat as Rollie prepared to write. "*Eliot was mostly to blame for my getting in trouble.*"

Rollie snapped his eyes up to her. He caught a glimmer in her unblinking eyes and a smile on the tip of her mouth.

"Rollin, I know Eliot got you trouble," she said in the softest tone he had heard her use yet, though still firm. "It was noble of you to take your punishment without ratting on him. Write the sentence. Once is sufficient. It will make you feel like justice was served. That's all for today." She waved her hand at him to go.

Still surprised, Rollie stumbled back, bumping into a desk. He turned and headed for the door.

"And Rollin?"

He turned around.

"You might add *fair* to your description of me."

He smiled. "Yes, Ms. Yardsly. Thank you."

For a moment, he thought he saw her wink!

CHAPTER 8

Pipes, Pens, and Ashes

The school's rooftop looked like an average recess area with tables and benches, a swing set, hopscotch courts, and even a plot of grass for field games. A tall chain link fence guarded the perimeter, and offered the students a great view of the neighborhood and nearby Regent's Park. Students sat at the tables, eating a morning snack. Some skip-roped, played hopscotch, or stood around chatting. Rollie spotted Cecily nibbling on toast at one table. Tibby sat next to her.

"Rollie, you're back fast!" Cecily exclaimed, spewing bread crumbs everywhere. "Was it awful?"

"No, Ms. Yardsly knew it wasn't all my fault. I had to write a sentence only once."

"That's nice of her. I didn't think she could be nice."

"We misjudged her. Are you ready for our next class?" He pulled out his little notepad. "Someone's class at ten-thirty in room D. That was the vial of dust."

"Right. I guess we'll know the teacher once we get there."

"Let's go. I feel better when I'm early."

"Me too." Cecily turned to Tibby. "Do you know what class you have?"

"I think the same one. I thought the same thing about those letters and numbers."

The three of them left the rooftop, taking the stairs back down to the second floor—quite a trek. They found room D filling up quickly. Apparently they were not the only students who liked to be early. They selected three seats in the second row. When the clock struck ten-thirty, all heads turned to the door in expectation of their teacher. They jumped with alarm when a woman's shrill voice exclaimed from the front of the room, "Ah-ha! Very interesting!"

A round stout woman popped her head up and crawled out from behind the desk on all fours, a magnifying glass in one chubby hand, and a familiar vial in the other. She scrambled to her feet and puffed. "You can find the most interesting particles to study in the tiniest cracks. Remember that, children! And welcome to...." She trailed off, setting down the magnifying glass and vial on her desk. Her short curly faded red hair frizzed at the ends. She wore men's trousers and a plain white blouse. Groping in her pockets, she foraged out a piece of chalk and turned to the blackboard. "Welcome to Identification of Fingerprint, Footprint, and Ash class." She wrote this on the board in curly but crooked cursive. "I am Amelia S. Hertz."

Rollie and Cecily glanced at each other with the same thought. That vial did not contain dust; it contained ash, the initials of Amelia's name.

"You may call me Miss Hertz. You may wonder why I am wearing men's trousers—yes, they're men's and I'm not ashamed to admit that. Well, children, in a skirt it is very difficult to crawl around on my hands and knees to study particles. So there. Are you in the right class? Hmm...I'll bet you'd like to know. Well, I'm not going to tell you. You must figure it out for yourself. I'm going to take a print of your right thumb. Then you have to match the print with one of those on that chart."

Everyone turned to a chart next to the door. The chart was divided into squares, each square displaying a black ink thumbprint.

"If you can match your thumbprint to one on the chart, then you're in this class. That's my class roster. I don't do well with names, but I never forget a fingerprint!" She rummaged around in her desk and found a large inkpad and a stack of white cards. She scurried around to each student and pressed his thumb onto the pad then onto the white card. When she came to Cecily, she sized her up with a smile. "You don't usually wear a dress, do you?"

"No, Miss Hertz. My mum made me because it's the first day of school. I usually wear my brother's trousers."

"I thought so. You didn't look comfortable. Well, there's no shame here, so you may wear those trousers if you like."

After thumb printed, Rollie took his white card to the chart and held it up to each print. He grew worried as he moved down the chart. Once he thought he had matched his, but then he looked more carefully and noticed a difference. Second to the last print, he stopped. He studied the two prints side by side. He was sure they matched. He remembered that on a class roster, Wilson would come last. He smiled and resumed his seat.

"Good, everyone matched! Well done for getting here! Let's begin class."

*   *   *   *

Eleven-thirty came too soon. Just as Rollie relaxed in Miss Hertz's class, he was dismissed to his next class. Rollie felt a little stressed, always hoping he had solved the class schedule correctly. So far, he and Cecily had proven their good detecting skills.

In room F, they selected similar seats as in the other two classrooms. As they sat down, they noticed their teacher sitting primly behind his desk, reading a book and smoking a pipe. He had white hair and a little white mustache. He looked very scholarly in his yellow tweed suit and bowtie. He cleared his throat every time he delicately turned a page. At eleven-thirty he checked the time on a gold pocket watch. He cleared his throat, closed his book, and stood. Puffing lightly on his pipe, he studied his students from beneath his bushy white eyebrows.

The students squirmed in their seats under his stare. A minute ticked by. Finally he took the pipe out of his mouth and cooed in a deep voice, "Etiquette. That's what this world needs more of. Someone tell me one good form of etiquette."

No one stirred.

"Come now, don't be bashful. Anyone?" he coaxed in a grandfatherly tone.

Slowly, Rollie raised his hand.

"Yes, lad?"

"Respecting our elders. Like calling them mister and madam."

"Very good, lad. That's positive social etiquette. Did you know that there is a level of etiquette for detectives? I am here to teach you that. This is my class entitled *Spy Etiquette and Interrogation.* I am Professor Ichabod P. Enches. It is good etiquette to address me as Professor Enches. I am the only faculty here with a doctorate degree. I have taught at several universities. I am privy to the title Professor, thus I require my students to address me in that way."

Rollie raised his hand slowly again.

"Yes, lad?"

"I have a note for you, Professor." Rollie pulled Mr. Crenshaw's letter from his inner coat pocket. He got to his feet and held it out to his teacher.

Professor Enches raised his bushy eyebrows in surprise. He reached out and took the letter. "Thank you, lad." He read his name on the envelope, and stuffed it into his outer coat pocket.

"It's from Mr.—"

"I know who it's from, thank you," Professor Enches acknowledged hurriedly. "Resume your seat." He coughed quietly. "Now, students, I will call roll, according to good class etiquette. If your name is not called, you must leave and find your class." He picked up a roll sheet from his desk and cleared his throat. "Brighton, Cecily A."

"Present!" Cecily called, thinking that was the polite way to respond.

Professor Enches nodded approvingly. He called the names, ending with Wilson, Rollin E. Everyone in the class responded to a name. Much to Rollie's dismay, he noticed Eliot sitting two seats behind him. Rollie made a mental note to stay clear of him.

After putting the roster away in a desk drawer, Professor Enches clasped his hands behind his back and stared at his students. Again his students squirmed in their seats.

"Can anyone tell me the usual method by which Sherlock Holmes encountered a mystery?"

Rollie's ears pricked up at the mention of his hero. He shot up his hand.

"Yes, Rollin?"

"Usually a client came to his apartment and told him about the mystery."

"Good. The proper term for that activity is House Meet," the professor informed, pointing at him. "Holmes always displayed a proper degree of etiquette while interviewing his clients. He also displayed etiquette while interrogating a suspect. That is what I will be teaching you in this class. Students, take notes." He turned his back on them to write on the blackboard. When he stepped away, the word *POLITENESS* stared back in capital letters.

The students looked inside their desks and found two pencils and a composition book. They took these out, and scribbled down *politeness* on the first page. For the rest of the hour, Professor Enches lectured on politeness. By the time lunch break came, the students felt like they had attended a college class.

*   *   *   *

Although Rollie grew a little drowsy after lunch, he was eager to attend his next class at one o'clock in room H. The pen represented this class. After selecting seats next to each, Rollie and Cecily leaned their heads together to discuss the day. They had not chatted at lunch because Headmaster Yardsly had made a welcome speech to the student body.

"We're doing great so far—guessing the class schedule and all," Rollie whispered.

"I love Miss Hertz!" Cecily squealed.

"Because she wears trousers?"

"Yes, and because she told me I could wear mine."

"How did she get our fingerprints on that chart?"

Cecily shrugged. "Maybe we left prints when we were here for orientation."

"What do you think about Professor Enches?"

Cecily snored. "Boring."

"I wish I knew what that letter from Mr. Crenshaw was all about."

Cecily nodded. "Professor Enches looked a little disturbed over it."

Rollie opened his mouth to comment, but stopped when the classroom door flew open. A man carrying an armload of rolled papers, notebooks, a mug of pencils, and a bulging leather briefcase barged into the room. His thick frizzy gray hair stood up on end, as if a mighty wind had swept past him. His green trousers and coat were wrinkled, one shoelace trailed untied, and his purple tie flapped over one shoulder. He blinked from behind super thick lenses magnifying his eyes. He resembled an owl. Sticking out his foot, the teacher tried to close the door, but leaned too much and spilled the pencils out of the mug. Tibby, who sat nearby, jumped up and gathered the pencils off the floor.

"Oh, thank you, little girl. Just put them right in this cup," he said in a high nervous voice. Once he had all the pencils again, he tried once more to close the door with his foot. The mug tipped precariously, ready to spill.

Tibby quickly closed the door before the pencils could fall from the cup.

"Thank you again. What's your name?" He bent down and peered into her face, too close for comfort.

Tibby stepped back and told her name.

"Wonderful, wonderful." He bustled to the front of the classroom, and dropped his armload onto the desk. Not bothering to tidy the desk, he stepped closer to the students. "Welcome, boys and girls. I teach Observation Level One. You must know that it is *very* – notice how I emphasized that word—*very* important to observe *everything*. Observing is different from seeing. Holmes saw everything that everyone else saw, but he trained himself to *notice* everything and deduce information from what he noticed. You may ask, 'Mr. Notch, how can I train myself?'" Here his voice rose to imitate a child.

"Well, I'll teach you soon enough, but first we must make sure you're in the right class. If you're not in the right class, you need to go find the right class. I do not take roll like other classes. 'But Mr. Notch, why do you not take roll?' you may ask," he squeaked. "I am counting on you to know if you're in the right class based on my own observations. I have had plenty of time to observe each of you today. 'I did not see you anywhere, Mr. Notch'. Ah, then I am a better detective than you probably thought. Now just sit tight, and I will read some of my observations. When you are sure that I am describing you, then call out 'Here!' or 'Present!' or anything else to let me know you are that person. Alrighty then."

Rollie and Cecily glanced at each other. Just when they thought they had met the most eccentric teacher who used the most unusual method of checking the roster, they met another one. Mr. Notch seemed the quirkiest.

"Nibbles bread, talks with her mouth full, uncomfortable in dresses, left-handed, freckles on nose, auburn—"

"That's me!" Cecily beamed.

"Right you are, Miss Brighton. Welcome to my class." Mr. Notch pushed his thick glasses up his nose and continued. "Missing a coat button, ink stains on right index finger, trims his crust, hazel eyes, reddish hair…"

Cecily tapped a boy's shoulder in front of her.

"Me?" the boy asked with some uncertainty.

Smiling, Mr. Notch affirmed, "Let's work on being more observant this year, Charlie B. Dover."

"I'll try, sir," Charlie mumbled.

Rollie figured that if Cecily was the first to be described, he had a while to wait until Mr. Notch got to him, since he had been at the end of all the rosters today. He guessed correctly.

"Hole in coat pocket, eats only hash browns for breakfast, short sandy-blond hair, excited brown eyes that—"

Rollie checked his coat pockets and gasped at a tiny hole in the left one. Mr. Notch kept reciting his observations until Rollie called, "Me!"

"That concludes our class roster. Welcome again, students. I have a little assignment for you all. In your desks you'll find some pencils and a composition book. Go ahead, take a peek. Those are for all your observation notes. You will take lots of notes. I want you to notice *everything*. Be sure to write down *everything*. Even little details that you think insignificant—write them down! Holmes knew the significance of details, for usually they were the key to solving the mystery. First assignment: observe someone in this room for five minutes and write down *everything*. You may begin."

Rollie swept his eyes around the room. They rested on Mr. Notch squirming behind his messy desk. Rollie jotted down a quick description of him. He described the desk and all the items on it. He put down his pencil. He picked it up again. He studied the briefcase closer. He noticed *Percy E. Notch* inscribed on the briefcase.

"PEN," he mumbled to himself with a smile.

CHAPTER 9

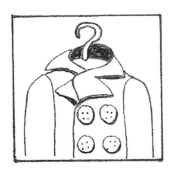

The Old Man and His Double

ℬefore Rollie knew it, an hour slipped by and hurried him onto his last class of the day at two o'clock in room G. He wondered how the teacher's name connected to the red ball cap.

Rollie and Cecily found room G down the hall from their other classrooms on the second floor. They dodged into the room and slipped into two seats. Behind them hobbled an extremely old man on shaky knees, bowed over a cane. A patch of snowy white hair sat atop his otherwise bald head. He wore a shabby sailor's pea-jacket, a frayed red scarf, stained white pants, and scuffed black shoes. He inched into the room, wheezing heavily. He took nearly three minutes to reach the front of the classroom. He turned slowly to face them, and smiled wearily. His face creased into a hundred wrinkles, but his blue eyes twinkled beneath bushy white eyebrows.

"Good afternoon, dear ones," he croaked in a faint voice. He wheezed a moment, and continued. "As ye can tell, I appear to be the oldest faculty member here. But one thing ye'll learn from me is that appearances can be deceiving." He paused to catch his breath. "Ye just came from Mr. Notch's Observation class, did ye not? Well then, observe me. Ye need not write anything down."

Rollie studied him closely. This teacher had to be older than his Auntie Ei; Rollie always regarded Auntie Ei as the oldest person he knew. As he moved his eyes over the old man, Rollie stopped at the teacher's hands grasping the cane. They contrasted with the rest of his appearance, for the hands bore no wrinkles, looking not much older than his brothers' hands. How strange! Rollie stared at the old sailor, wondering if maybe…

"Close yer eyes, children. Tight. No peeking."

Rollie closed his eyes, his curiosity building. He listened to the sounds of rubber peeling, something sticky becoming unstuck, and the cane rattling on the floor.

"You can look, kids!" a young man's voice announced in a strong American accent.

When he opened his eyes, Rollie gasped at the young man standing before him. He had black wavy hair and bright blue eyes. His face was pleasant with normal features. He was the type of man that Rollie thought he would see in any crowd anywhere. The young teacher mashed something flesh-colored and sticky in his hands.

"Like I said, appearances can be deceiving. Just a little stage makeup, fake hair, and some great acting, if I say so myself, and you have an ancient sailor before you. Want to take a guess as to which class I teach? Yes?"

"Some sort of disguise class?" Cecily piped up.

"Bingo! I teach the Art of Disguise Level One. Just between you and me, this is the most fun class in the whole school." He leaned in towards the students and whispered, "But don't tell any of the other teachers. They might get jealous and fire me."

The teacher grinned. "I'm kidding! But seriously, this is a fun class. Want to guess my name?"

"Do your initials spell out cap?" Rollie guessed.

The young man's features grew solemn as he rushed over to Rollie. "How did you know that? Are you a spy?"

"No, sir, I—"

"Good guess, kid!" he exclaimed, patting Rollie on the back. "I surely hope you're in my class. Are you in my class?"

"I hope so, sir."

"In that case," he whispered into Rollie's ear, "my name is Chadwick A. Permiter." He jogged back to the front of the room. "Now, class, there is someone among us at this moment who knows my name."

He paused dramatically and announced like a circus master, "Will that person please stand up and tell the rest of the class my name?"

Rollie shot to his feet. He already loved this teacher who had more energy than he did. "Chadwick A. Permiter!"

Mr. Permiter clapped his hands enthusiastically. "Wonderful performance, young man. If you are not in this class, I strongly encourage you to go join the London Theatre Troup. Perhaps you'll make a very convincing Macbeth. Anyways," he continued casually, waving his hand as if sweeping away that conversation. "Are you ready to have some fun? Are you ready to see through disguises and catch some bad guys? Are you ready to don a disguise and become a hero? Don't look so surprised, that's what this whole detective business is about. Are you ready?"

The students nodded and fidgeted in their seats with excitement.

"Great! First we gotta make sure you're supposed to be here. I'm gonna do this in a quick, painless way—like ripping off a band-aid. Is there anyone here named Herbie Z. Frecklebottom?" He searched earnestly around the room.

The children stifled giggles.

"No? Well, that's the only student who is not supposed to be here. I know that everyone else is in the right place." He spun around to the blackboard, but then spun back around. "By the way, if anyone does run into Herbie Z. Frecklebottom, please tell him the principal—I mean, *headmaster*— wants to see him."

At the second mention of this ridiculous name, all the students openly giggled.

Mr. Permiter put his hands on his hips. "How dare you laugh at poor Herbie Frecklebottom! He comes from the prestigious Frecklebottom and Wartnose families!"

The children roared with laughter. For a moment Mr. Permiter held his serious composure, but then burst out laughing with them. "Just kidding. There are no such people—at least not here. I can't speak for the rest of the world. See? I love to have fun, but I'm also serious about learning. It will be advantageous for you to know when to kid and when to be serious. I'll help you out with that." Mr. Permiter hopped onto his desk and sat cross-legged atop it. "Let's discuss my disguise. Did anyone see through it? Be honest. Don't sound smart just to impress me. It *will* work." He winked at them. "Yes, Rollie?"

Rollie widened his eyes in surprise at the mention of his name.

"Yes, I know your names already. Put your hand down, Rollie."

Rollie smiled. "I noticed your hands. They didn't look old."

Mr. Permiter snapped his fingers. "A dead give-away. Good one, Rollie!"

"Thank you, Mr. Permiter."

"You can call me Mr. Chad. But not you." He pointed to a little girl right in front of him. When she looked crestfallen, he grinned. "Kidding! You may all call me Mr. Chad."

"Mr. Chad? I noticed something else."

"Let's have it, Rollie."

"That old sailor disguise was the same one that Sherlock Holmes wore in *The Sign of the Four*."

"Bingo! A true Sherlockian! If I didn't know any better, I'd say you were a detective. Now to tell you a little bit about myself," Mr. Chad began, as if someone had just asked him about his life. "I'm American, grew up in New York City, and yes, it is a grand city, and yes, I am personal friends with Lady Liberty. A year ago, I came here to teach. I'm still the new kid on the block, so to speak. I love the Brits, but hate your food. It's very boring. And I refuse to wear a tie." He pointed to his collar. "Professor Enches always gives me a hard time and tells me it's professional etiquette to wear a tie." He shrugged. "One last thing I will tell you: this school is full of mysteries, so keep a wary eye out!"

*   *   *   *

"I think Mr. Chad is my favorite teacher," Rollie said as he and Cecily skipped downstairs.

"He is very funny. I like his accent, but Miss Hertz is my favorite."

They reached the downstairs hall where a line had formed. The students waited turns to read the dormitory assignment on the wall. Some moans of disappointment and some squeals of excitement could be heard as students read with whom they would room.

"My head feels like it's going to explode!" Rollie exclaimed. "I'm so tired but so excited. I'm going to love being here."

"Me too! Especially since Mr. Chad said there are plenty of mysteries here."

"I think I already know one."

"Really? Oh, that letter from Mr. Crenshaw."

"Yes. It could be nothing, but you never know." Rollie shrugged.

"It's at least mysterious that Mr. Crenshaw had you deliver it."

Rollie edged up to the list tacked on the wall. He found his name. "I'm in room O on the fourth floor. I'm rooming with...Oh no! Eliot! And some other boy named Rupert."

"You don't like Eliot?"

"Do you? He's annoying. Where are you?"

Cecily used her finger to track down her name. "I'm on the third floor in room J. I'm with Tibby and Margot."

They scooted out of the way and mounted the stairs.

"What about our normal studies?" Rollie asked, clutching the banister.

"You mean grammar and history and all that?"

"Do we know when those classes are?"

"I think they'll let us know," Cecily panted as they mounted the second floor stairs.

They did not say another word as they climbed. Cecily waved goodbye on the third floor, and Rollie continued on up to the fourth. On the fourth floor, the hallway bustled with boys. Two tall boys tossed a yellow ball to each other. Another three boys chased each other in and out of open rooms. More boys bumped past each other, trying to find their rooms. Rollie found his at the end of the hallway. The door gaped open. When he stepped inside, he spotted Eliot leaning out the one window. The room was small with three beds lined against three of the walls. One desk stood under the window, which made Rollie grimace; he had hoped for his own desk instead of having to share one with two other roommates. Rollie found his suitcase, boxes, and book bag stacked on the bed nearest the door. He strode over and opened a suitcase.

Eliot turned. "Hello, roomie."

"Hello," Rollie mumbled.

"Glad to be rooming with you. I was nervous I'd be rooming with someone I didn't know."

"What's Rupert like?"

Eliot shrugged. "He hasn't been up yet. It's great that we have classes together, too. Although I thought we'd be in all the same classes because we're both new students. That's the way it should be. All new students should take the same classes together."

"Another rule you have?"

"It should be a rule. What other classes are you taking?"

Rollie draped his bathrobe over the end of his bed. "Probably the same ones you're taking, but at different times. Do you know anything about our extra classes? For math and grammar and all that?"

"They didn't tell you? That's what they call *independent studies*." Eliot opened the deep bottom desk drawer. "All your text books are in here. We follow a syllabus. We have to do it in our own time. I'm thinking if I get up early I can do a few subjects before breakfast. That way I'll have more free time in the afternoon. Plus I want to use the desk first. I hope you don't mind. I set my alarm for five o'clock."

Rollie groaned. "Five o'clock! That's so early. Why don't you study in the library?"

"It's all the way downstairs," Eliot protested. "I'll be really quiet. Actually you should wake up and study with me."

"No, thanks. I work better in the afternoon."

"You should get it done in the morning."

"Don't tell me what to do," Rollie snapped. His head swam with the events of the day. He needed a little peace to settle his thoughts.

Eliot held up his palms in a gesture of defense. "Cranky! I'm just trying to be a good chum."

"Sorry, Eliot. My head is so full right now."

"I know what you mean. You know what I do to relax? I read my comic books."

"Who do you read?"

"Sherlock Holmes."

"Sherlock Holmes comic books?"

"My grandpa gives them to me. They're really rare." Eliot tossed his pillow aside and grabbed a small stack of black and white comic books. "You can borrow them whenever you want. Start with this one." He held up one titled *The Adventure of the Speckled Band.*

"I love that mystery!" Rollie took the comic book and lay down on his bed. At first, Eliot appeared to be an unpleasant person, but maybe he would not be such a bad roommate after all.

CHAPTER 10

Rollie the Postman

By Friday, Rollie grew accustomed to his new school. He memorized his schedule, regained his appetite, and slept through the night. Surprisingly, Eliot studied quietly in the wee hours of the morning, using a flashlight to read by. Rupert kept to himself, being a boy with a solemn face; he never appeared happy to be there.

But Rollie was.

He liked having different teachers for different subjects; he felt like one of his father's college students. He liked that the teachers never gave homework. He liked that most of class time was used for practicing things, instead of listening to things—except for Professor Enches, who enjoyed lecturing in a boring manner. Rollie deemed Mr. Chad his favorite. Mr. Chad often called on Rollie to answer questions, or used Rollie to demonstrate applying a false nose or eyebrows. Rollie found him interesting and loved listening to his American accent. Rollie had never been this excited about school—not even with Mrs. Simmons.

Late Friday morning, Rollie sat listening to Professor Enches ramble on about the polite manner to introduce oneself to a potential client. Rollie took notes diligently, but after thirty minutes, his mind wandered. He thought about his family and what it would be like returning home for the weekend later that afternoon. He hoped his brothers would not tease him too much, but he did hope his family asked lots of questions about his week. He hoped the dinner conversation centered on him—he did not hope too high though.

"Always make direct eye contact. This is not only polite, but also assertive, showing your client that you are interested, attentive, and courageous to hear whatever frightful tale they are about to disclose to you."

Rollie heard Professor Enches in the background, so twitched with surprise when he felt the professor brush past him. An envelope landed on his desk with a light slap. Professor Enches continued walking down the rows of desks, not bothering to look back. Rollie read the front: *To Mr. Crenshaw, M.U.S.*

A response to Mr. Crenshaw's first letter? Did Professor Enches mean for Rollie to deliver this? *"This school is full of mysteries, so keep a wary eye out!"* Was this one of those mysteries? Surely it was. Did Mr. Chad know something about this?

Rollie shook his head. He probably made this out to be a bigger deal than it was. Probably just a friendly correspondence between two friends. But why did Rollie have to be their postman?

As soon as class was dismissed, Rollie leaped to his feet and dodged through his classmates to Professor Enches' desk. The professor sorted through his notes. When he spotted Rollie heading for him, he quickly turned to erase the blackboard.

"Professor, sir, did you—"

"I've no time for your questions, lad. If you need additional notes, speak with a classmate," the professor mumbled, nose to the blackboard.

"No, it's not about class. This envelope you—"

"Do not be impertinent, young man. I am very busy and you are late for lunch. Hurry along this instant or I shall report you to Headmaster Yardsly." Professor Enches turned around and shooed Rollie towards the door.

Rollie stepped out as the door slammed in his face. He stood blinking at it for a moment. That confirmed it—something mysterious surrounded this envelope. He tucked it into his trouser pocket and hurried off to lunch.

*   *   *   *

"Rollie, tell us all about your first week of school!" his mother exclaimed at the dinner table later that evening.

"Solve any big cases yet?" Edward snickered through a mouthful of potatoes.

"Rooming with any villains?" Stewart added.

"Boys," Mrs. Wilson warned. "Let Rollie speak."

"It's great, mum, I really love it!"

"Whoa!" Stewart commented. "The kid's eyes just got really wide when he said that!"

"He must be pretty excited!" Edward gasped dramatically.

"What are the classes like?" Mr. Wilson spoke up, regarding Rollie over his spectacles.

"It's like college, dad. One of my teachers is actually a professor."

"Who is he? Maybe I know him."

"Professor Enches."

"Enches?"

"Professor Ichabod P. Enches."

"Ichabod? Very odd name."

"His initials spell PIPE."

Mr. Wilson chewed thoughtfully on his roasted chicken. Then his face lit up. "PIPE! Wasn't that one of the items in your hollow book?"

"Yeah! Dad, it's so clever. All those items were the initials of all my teachers, and—"

"That *is* clever!" Stewart exclaimed.

"What item am I?" Edward asked. "What's an EPW?"

"Nothing. But I'm SAW. Ha!" Stewart socked his twin in the shoulder.

"Boys, we're listening to Rollie," Mrs. Wilson cut in.

"Fact: I don't know any Enches," Mr. Wilson continued. "Never heard of an Enches. Where did he get his degree?"

Rollie shrugged. "I don't know. He said he taught at several universities."

"Which ones?"

"He didn't say. Oh! One of my teachers is American. He's from New York City."

"New York City!" Edward exclaimed. "Lucky bloke! Someday I'm going to New York City."

"You'll never go. It's too expensive," Stewart said matter-of-factly.

"I want to see the Statue of Liberty!" Lucille piped up. "She's really tall."

"Lady Liberty," Daphne chimed in.

From that point on, the conversation never returned to Rollie, but he was not disappointed—he had not hoped too high.

After dinner, the family went their separate ways. Rollie headed upstairs, anxious to be in his room again. As he passed Auntie Ei's bedroom, he heard a distinct clearing of the throat. He poked his head in her doorway. The old woman sat in her comfy armchair next to a glowing fireplace. She appeared to be reading.

"Did you want something, Auntie Ei?"

"You were not able to tell us much at the dinner table tonight." She kept her eyes on her book.

"That's okay. I'm used to it."

"Is it a fine school? Are you studying hard?" Her eyes did not look up as she turned a page.

"Yes, Auntie. I really love it." Rollie ventured into the bedroom. He had set foot in that room only two other times before: once to collect some ashes from her fireplace to study under his magnifying glass, and another time to read to her when she fell ill. The first time he got scolded, and the second time he got thanked. He wondered what he would get this time. "One teacher said the school was full of mysteries. That got me excited."

Her eyes snapped up to meet him. "Mysteries? What kinds of mysteries?"

"I don't know yet, Auntie."

"Well, keep a wary eye all the same." Her eyes dropped back down to her book.

"That's what Mr. Chad told me."

"Is he the American teacher?"

"Yes. He's really fun."

"Americans generally are, but they also have strange ideals. Beware of him."

Rollie felt a little shaken by this last comment. He had never thought to beware of any teacher, least of all Mr. Chad.

"Did you like the marmalade? I hope you did not throw out the jar. It may be useful."

Rollie had forgotten about his great-aunt's odd gift. "I haven't eaten any yet," he confessed in a small voice.

"Well, you should enjoy it soon before it goes bad. In the library at school, perhaps."

"That's what your label said."

"Can you think of a better place for snacking on marmalade?"

Rollie did not know how to answer the question, for it was ridiculous, just like the marmalade. "I'll try some this week."

"It's of no consequence." More to herself she mumbled, "At this point, anyway."

Rollie caught that last statement. He watched his old great-aunt sitting cozily by the fire, book in lap. She appeared a simple person, but appearances could be deceiving, as Rollie had learned so far. For the first time, Rollie grew suspicious of his great-aunt. Suspicious she knew more than she let on. Suspicious she had a connection to his new school. And suspicious she had a different purpose for giving him the jar of marmalade.

*   *   *   *

Rollie poised his finger inches from the doorbell. He fingered the envelope with his left hand. He never thought he would ever stand on this porch. He always thought of this house as forbidden land, visiting it only through his telescope. He pushed the doorbell.

From inside he heard the *clip-clop, clip-clop* of heels upon marble floors. The door opened.

"Good afternoon," the young brassy-haired secretary greeted in a pleasant voice with a pleasant expression on her pretty face. "May I help you?"

With a gulp, Rollie answered, "I have a letter for Mr. Crenshaw." He held it out to her.

"Would you like to deliver it yourself?" she asked in a musical tone.

"Um, I guess."

"Follow me."

Clip-clop, clip-clop. He followed her through the house—a very grand house with high ceilings decorated with Italian frescos. The secretary led him to the back patio. Mr. Crenshaw sat in his usual spot under the willow tree. He rose to his feet as Rollie stepped outside.

"Good afternoon, young neighbor. How are you today?" He extended one of his gloved hands.

"Fine, thank you." Rollie shook it, and held out the envelope to him.

Mr. Crenshaw took it with a nod. "I am much obliged. I hope you do not mind being our little postman. We are old acquaintances who have recently reconnected. We do not know each others' addresses."

"Oh, that's okay. I could exchange addresses for you."

"Don't bother. The post is…well, so slow these days. We prefer your quick delivery. If you don't mind, that is."

"I don't mind."

"Thank you very much. You are an obliging lad. Tell me, how are you enjoying Sherlock Academy?"

"Very much. Do you know about my school, sir?"

"Oh, yes, my nephew attended there many years ago. I paid for his tuition. I wonder if it has changed much. Who is the present headmaster?"

"Headmaster Yardsly."

"How many students attend?"

"Not sure. I'd say about eighty. The dorm list had about that many names on it."

"That's a good number. How many faculty members?"

"There are six including the headmaster."

"It sounds like the school is prospering," Mr. Crenshaw commented to himself in a somewhat uneasy tone. "Have you solved the rearranging library yet?"

Rollie opened his mouth to answer, but stopped himself. A change had come over Mr. Crenshaw. The elderly man peered intently at him from beneath a furrowed brow. His tone had shifted from friendly inquiring to pressing interrogation. Rollie felt uneasy.

"I better be going, sir."

Mr. Crenshaw blinked and eased his gaze. Back to a friendly voice, he said, "Of course, young man. Thank you again for your service. Good luck to you in school. My secretary will show you out."

Rollie followed the petite secretary back through the house and out the front door. As he headed home, he decided he preferred visiting Mr. Crenshaw through the telescope.

CHAPTER 11

The Silent Library

"*He* gave you another letter?

"Yep. M.U.S. pops up again." Rollie pointed to the initials next to Professor Enches' name on the envelope.

"You went to his house? Was it odd?" Cecily peppered, wide-eyed.

"It was," Rollie admitted. "I felt really uncomfortable. He asked me a lot of questions about Sherlock Academy."

They sat side by side in the horse-drawn cab. It was a foggy Monday morning, typical of England, but disappointing to summer vacationers. The hansom bounced along towards London.

"You said his nephew used to go there. I wonder who he was?"

"Mr. Crenshaw paid for his tuition."

"That's nice. Well, we know he *is* awfully rich." Cecily gasped. "Maybe *he's* your anonymous donor!"

Rollie shook his head. "That makes no sense. He hardly knows me."

"He knew you were attending the school. That's why he gave you the first letter to deliver. How did he know? Who told him?"

"Maybe my parents. Dad talks to him once in awhile," Rollie shrugged.

"Why would he trust you as his postman? He has another motive for that. I wouldn't rule him out entirely."

"I'll consider it. Right now it doesn't matter who my donor is. I'd like to know, but I don't *have* to."

Within fifteen minutes, the cab pulled up beside 221 Baker Street. Rollie and Cecily both looked around in confusion as they stepped out. The front steps of the school were bustling with people. A squad of blue uniformed policemen patrolled the front doors, keeping nosy neighbors from entering the building. A few other students who had just arrived stood on the curb, not sure what to do.

"What happened here?" Cecily wondered.

Rollie led her to a nearby bobby. "Excuse me, sir, may we enter?"

The bobby glared down at him. "Are you a student?"

"Yes, sir, we all are," Rollie answered, indicating Cecily and the three other students nearby.

"Very well, go ahead." The bobby nodded toward the front doors. "Stoaky! Let these children pass!"

Stoaky, guarding the doors, stepped aside to allow the children through. The entry hall was no quieter than outside. Several plainclothes inspectors—Rollie guessed from Scotland Yard—stood around interviewing staff and writing notes.

"Do you have night security?" one tall inspector, a fedora pushed back on his head, asked the headmaster.

"No, there's never been a need," Headmaster Yardsly replied, shaking his head sadly. Noticing the new arrivals, he turned and told them, "First classes are postponed. There's an assembly on the roof in ten minutes." He turned back to the inspectors.

"What do you think happened here?" Cecily whispered.

Rollie went on tiptoes, trying to see past the inspector and the headmaster. Beyond them a few more policemen lingered around the library. "I think we're about to find out. Let's head to the roof." He led the others upstairs.

Along their way up the four flights of stairs, they bumped into a few policement. Some asked students a few questions, some measured the halls, and some photographed the windows. On the roof, the children found the student body and faculty sitting at picnic tables. A podium stood before them. Rollie and Cecily found seats next to Tibby and Eliot.

"Pretty exciting, huh?" Eliot poked Rollie in the ribs.

"I guess. What happened?"

"A mystery! And we've got to solve it!"

"*We* do?"

"Sure. Between you and me, I think this is all a set up to give us some field experience."

"It's a pretty elaborate set up," Rollie muttered doubtfully.

"Want to be my partner?"

"You're getting ahead of yourself. We had better wait to hear from Headmaster Yardsly before we pick partners."

"Hey," Cecily cut in. "I'm Rollie's partner."

"Tibby, want to be partners?" Eliot asked, leaning over Rollie to speak with the girl.

Tibby glanced at him nervously. She started to say something, but Headmaster Yardsly interrupted. He stood behind his podium.

"SLEUTHS!" his voice boomed, demanding everyone's attention. Back to a normal pitch, he continued, "A burglary has been committed here at Sherlock Academy. An *attempted* burglary, mind you. Never in the history of our school has there been an attempted burglary—well, at least not one fabricated by our staff. That's right, this is not a mock crime for fieldwork. This is the real deal, if you will." He paused and took a sip of water from a glass he kept behind the podium.

The students whispered their speculations to each other.

"AHEM!" Headmaster Yardsly yelled, more as a word than an actual clearing of his throat. "Let's stop the gossip. All you need to know is that the library was broken into last night, but nothing was taken. We will have a couple bobbies patrolling the grounds at night. You are dismissed to your regular classes!"

The students scrambled to their feet and filed downstairs where they dispersed to their classrooms. Since it was only nine-fifteen, Rollie, Cecily, and Eliot headed to Ms. Yardsly's class. There Ms. Yardsly posted herself behind her desk. Her hands rested on two tall stacks of books. An unusual amount of chatter filled the classroom as the students took their seats.

"Quiet, students, quiet!" Ms. Yardsly ordered, eyeing them with her cold stare. "I do not want to hear another word about the burglary. We are here to learn codes and ciphers. I have your textbooks. They just arrived by post yesterday. I need two volunteers."

Whenever Ms. Yardsly asked for volunteers, nobody raised a hand. Everyone felt nervous about helping, afraid the helper might do the wrong thing under her watchful eyes. Ms. Yardsly commissioned her own volunteers.

"Rollin E. Wilson! Eliot S. Tildon! Quickly, quickly, don't dawdle!"

The two boys bustled up to her desk.

"Each take a stack of textbooks and distribute them to your classmates." She turned to the blackboard and feverishly scribbled a code on it. She always wrote with such fervor, oftentimes breaking her chalk.

Rollie and Eliot struggled to grip the tall stack of heavy textbooks. They held them in their arms, steadying the stacks under their chins. They moved around the classroom, squatting a bit so each student could take a book. They kept the last books for themselves and returned to their desks without incident.

Whew! Rollie breathed, glad nothing embarrassing had happened, glad Ms. Yardsly had kept her eyes on the board and not on him.

Ms. Yardsly spun around. "Cecily A. Brighton! Please read the title of our textbook aloud."

Cecily licked her lips. *"On Secret Writings: One Hundred Sixty Separate Ciphers."* She gasped, and added, "Sherlock Holmes wrote this!"

"You are correct. It is one of his many monographs. Turn to page seven."

The flipping of pages could be heard.

Rollie felt a little overwhelmed as he thumbed through the 325-page textbook filled with jumbles of letters and numbers. He closed his eyes. All he wanted to think about was the burglary. It had shaken him up, to think the school was not entirely safe. But it had also heightened his detective senses. He liked having a real mystery to solve. He hoped to do a little investigation of his own, which got him thinking...

Why would someone commit a burglary, but not steal anything? Was the thief interrupted before he could steal? Why the library? Nothing but books there. All the shelves rearranged themselves every twenty-four hours. Hmm…why *did* the shelves rearrange every twenty-four hours? A security procedure? Maybe there was something valuable in the library after all…

Rollie tried to concentrate the last fifteen minutes of class. Too hard. Finally Ms. Yardsly dismissed them to recess. Last week Rollie had made friends with Wesley Livingston, a fourth year rugby captain, who let him play in a match. He thought of joining the team in another game today, but he had an urge to visit the library. He wove his way downstairs against the flow of traffic. He entered the library.

The light was off, so the room was very dim. A board against the window blocked weak sunlight. Rollie noticed the pane had been broken. He tiptoed across the room to the lamp on the side table. He pulled its chain to turn it on. The soft glow melted away any spookiness he felt. He stared long and hard at the walls of tall bookcases. He swept his eyes along one shelf at his eye-level. The titles varied, randomly.

The Complete Poems of Edgar Allan Poe.

A Child's Garden of Verses.

The History of the Airplane and Other Flying Machines.

Art History: Renaissance.

Pollyanna.

Rollie wondered where his beloved Sherlock Holmes book slept. He counted the bookcases lining the walls: eight, about four feet across, and towering up to the ceiling. He remembered watching the books slide and drop and raise and get all mixed up. He felt a little hopeless as he perused the hundreds of books and imagined them shuffling around soon. Rollie wondered if any of the other students, especially the upperclassmen, had found their books. He assumed most of the other students had brought Sherlock Holmes volumes too. If he were right, he could expect to find at least a few Holmes books. He stepped up to a center bookcase and ran his finger and eyes down each stack of books.

He reached the bottom shelf when he heard the bell faintly from the rooftop, signaling recess over. He quickly checked the last books on the bottom shelf, flicked off the lamp, then bounded upstairs to his next class. He puzzled over what he had found, or rather what he had *not* found: any Sherlock Holmes books.

CHAPTER 12

Eighty Missing Holmes

"*I* apologize for being a few minutes delayed," Professor Enches announced as he hurried into the classroom. His long legs took him to the front in barely six strides. "The disturbing events of last night had me detained. I will say no more. Tardiness is a form of poor etiquette. However, if it is due to imperative detective work, it is somewhat justified. If you are ever tardy due to a case, be sure to express that to your client, and apologize sincerely. Proceed to present the fruit of your tardiness, so they can see its justification. Understand?"

The students had learned it was unnecessary to answer his questions, which were frequently rhetorical. Of course they understood, or at least tried to understand, but they did not need to assure him of that. Expecting no answer, Professor Enches found his pipe in his pocket, scratched a match on his sole, and lit the pipe. After a few puffs, he nodded in satisfaction, then stared at his students for a few moments, a ritual he practiced every class period.

Remembering Mr. Crenshaw's second letter in his pocket, Rollie raised his hand.

Professor Enches puffed on his pipe and nodded at Rollie, indicating permission to speak.

"I have another letter for—"

Professor Enches coughed gruffly, took two strides over to Rollie, and snatched the letter from his outstretched hand. "Thank you, lad. Please see me after class." He stuffed the envelope into his outer coat pocket and returned to the front. "Students, today we will discuss correct etiquette when interviewing a client of the opposite gender. If you were a male, then a client of the opposite gender would be a female, and vice versa. Now let's suppose that a client enters your office and…"

Please see me after class…

Those words pounded in Rollie's ears. Was he in trouble? For what? Delivering Mr. Crenshaw's letters? Surely not—that would be unjust. Rollie wished Professor Enches' lecture would hurry by, but of course it did not. Along with most children, Rollie found that whenever he anticipated something, time slowed, making the wait unbearable. Yet whenever Rollie reached that anticipated moment, time sped up, ending the excitement too soon. Since Rollie anticipated something unpleasant, he hoped the rule held true, that his anticipated conversation with the professor would speed by.

Class ended, students dispersed to lunch, and Rollie waited for Professor Enches. Cecily raised her eyebrows at Rollie, wondering what could be the matter this time. She ducked out the door. The professor stepped up to Rollie.

"Lad, I thank you for delivering Mr. Crenshaw's and my correspondences. However, it is poor etiquette to interrupt class to deliver those letters to me in front of your peers. I would appreciate it if you would drop the letters on my desk before class commences. That would be the most polite procedure. Is that clear?"

Not accustomed to answering the professor, Rollie blinked at him.

"Is that clear, lad?"

"Oh, yes. I'll drop the letter on your desk before class."

Professor Enches puffed and nodded. "Thank you. Dismissed."

*   *   *   *

Students filled the tables on the roof, eating their lunches and chatting with their friends. Most conversations revolved around the attempted burglary. Rollie smiled gratefully at Cecily as he slid into a seat she had saved for him.

"In trouble again? That's not like you," Cecily commented between bites of her sandwich.

Rollie leaned in and whispered. "It was about Mr. Crenshaw's letters. It was nothing." He unwrapped his sandwich and unscrewed his milk bottle cap, a lunch provided by the school. He bit, chewed, swallowed, and asked the other students at the table, "Did any of you bring Sherlock Holmes as your favorite book for orientation?"

All twelve students at the table nodded as they chewed.

Rollie's eyebrows shot up. "And all of you put your books in the rearranging library?"

More nodding and chewing.

"Have any of you found your book yet?"

Now their heads shook.

"Have you?" Eliot piped up, concern in his eyes.

"No, but I want to."

Eliot looked relieved.

"How many students are enrolled here?" Rollie asked.

A tall lanky girl squinted her eyes in thought. "I think there's around eighty."

"That was my guess. How long have you been here?"

"This is my fourth year—my last."

"I thought so. You look older than us."

The tall girl smiled. "I'm fourteen."

Rollie chewed thoughtfully. "Do you know any students who *didn't* bring a Sherlock Holmes book?"

She squinted her eyes again. "Now that I think about it, no."

"Interesting."

Cecily giggled. "Rollie, there's nothing interesting about *that*. It's no surprise that students would bring a Sherlock Holmes book to *Sherlock* Academy. Even if they didn't read much Holmes, any smart student would bring one anyway. Everyone wants to fit in."

Cecily was right about that—Rollie did not find that interesting. Eighty copies of Sherlock Holmes—now *that* was interesting. He jumped to his feet, stuffing the last of his sandwich into his mouth and draining the last of his milk.

"Where are you going?" Cecily questioned.

"I've got some work to catch up on."

Eliot pointed an accusing finger at him. "I *told* you that you should get your work done in the mornings. It's the best time."

Rollie rolled his brown eyes. "See you in class." He darted across the roof before anyone else could pester him. He skipped down four flights of stairs, arriving at the library out of breath. He paused in the doorway to slow his breathing. He spotted Mr. Notch bumbling down the hall towards him. His arms grappled with his briefcase, papers, and mug of pencils, as usual.

"Hello, Mr. Notch."

Mr. Notch stumbled to a halt, not seeing Rollie until he nearly bumped into the boy. "Oh, hello, hello. Rollin, is it? Thank goodness I remembered. I can be very absent-minded. You know, not remembering little things. I try so hard to remember names. How are you today?"

"Fine, thank you. Just thought I'd take a try at the rearranging library."

"Did you now? Good, good. Would you like a hint?"

Rollie's eyes brightened. "I sure would!"

"Of course you would. Who wouldn't want a hint? Keep one thing in mind: things are not what they seem on the outside." He attempted to tap his nose to gesture smartness, but found he had no free hands. He almost dropped his pencil mug in the attempt. "Oh! Never mind, I'm sure you get the idea. I'm off to class."

"What time is it?" Rollie asked with a hint of panic.

"Don't worry. You still have twenty minutes. I try to get to class early so I don't have to come in juggling all this." He smiled, blinked behind his ultra thick glasses, and staggered down the hall towards the staircase.

By now Rollie had found his breath, so he stepped into the library and pulled the lamp chain. He decided to work from one end of the room to the other. He hurried to the far left bookcase. He had to stand on tiptoe to see the top shelves. As he worked down the books, he got quicker at reading the titles. Within a few minutes, he reached the bottom shelf and finished checking that bookcase. He moved on to the second bookcase. Racing his eyes and fingers, he finished checking all eight bookcases before the bell rang. He plopped down on the floor between two shelves, resting his head against the wall. Two-foot spaces separated the bookcases from each other.

Rollie sighed. A mystery burrowed in his mind: there were no Sherlock Holmes books found on any of the eight bookcases. Where were all the students' books? The students had placed their books on shelves, watched them get shuffled around, and lost sight of them. Obviously, they had lost sight of them because—

"They disappeared." Rollie shook his head in bewilderment.

How could eighty books disappear? Did the headmaster take them? What for? Did he have them for safekeeping? Would he return them? And what—

"—Is that a hole?"

Rollie widened his eyes with excitement, like when he had first read his invitation to the school, or when he had figured out the class schedule. And there it was—that flutter in his middle. He was not sure what he just discovered, but he felt it was something important.

Rollie scrambled to his feet and peered into a hole in the side of the bookcase on his left. It was not too deep or too large a hole. Gingerly, he stuck his hand in the hole, feeling the width and height and depth. He felt a raised shape sticking out of from the backing. He traced it with his fingers. It felt like the number eight. He retrieved his hand and studied the side of the opposite bookcase on his right. Another similar hole. He fingered the inside—a seven, he guessed.

What fit into those holes? The holes were a little bigger than a toilet paper roll. Smaller than a paint can. More like the size of...

A jar!

Ring! Ring!

Lunch recess ended. Rollie groaned, but stuck his hand in one more hole in another bookcase—a six. Bouncing with excitement, he sprinted out the library, forgetting to turn off the lamp. He took the stairs two at a time. Panting, he rushed into class and took his seat. He turned to Cecily next to him, but she would not look at him. Rollie glanced at Mr. Notch's desk: no teacher, no briefcase or papers, and no pencil mug.

At that moment, Mr. Notch burst into the room, his arms still full of everything he had carried earlier. As he passed Rollie, he grinned sheepishly.

"There's always something!"

CHAPTER 13

A Jarring Clue

Although Rollie enjoyed Mr. Notch's class, he had come to look forward to Mr. Chad's class, which promised interesting disguises and funny anecdotes. Today's class did not disappoint.

"So what gave me away this time?" Mr. Chad grinned at his students, scratching his neck beneath a red cravat. "Cecily!"

"You're wearing your saddle-shoes. I don't think a common loafer would wear saddle-shoes."

"Bingo! Like hands, shoes can be dead-give-aways, too. Now this woman I knew who worked in a New York department store told me that shoes could either make or break an outfit. Does anyone know what that means? Tibby!"

"My older sis says that, too. It means shoes can make an outfit look good or bad."

"Bright as a penny! Or pence, I guess. While that is true, not too many people notice a person's shoes. But you're all bright detectives, so there was no fooling you!" He wiggled out of a shiny seedy coat, the collar turned up. Next he whipped off his cap and red cravat. He tossed the whole disguise into a costume box he kept in the corner by his desk. He sat cross-legged atop his desk. "Let's review: nose-hairs and earlobes can give a disguise away, right?"

The students giggled and shook their heads.

"No? What can give disguises away? Hands and…?"

"Shoes!" everyone chimed.

"I'm so proud!" Mr. Chad gushed, wiping away imaginary tears from his twinkling blue eyes. "By the way, the fun thing about a disguise like that one—" He pointed to the ragged coat, red cravat, and cap in the corner. "—Is that you can be any type of worker or loafer. Maybe you're looking for work as a carpet layer, a plumber, a napkin-stasher….Oh, there is such a job."

Rollie smiled. Yes, Mr. Chad was his favorite, but being a polite boy, Rollie would never tell Mr. Chad that; he did not want to hurt the other teachers' feelings.

"Extra points if you can identify that loafer disguise!"

Hands flashed up.

"Eliot?"

"Holmes wore it in *The Adventure of the Blue Carbuncle*."

"I can't teach you smarties anything more today. Class dismissed!"

Mr. Chad always stood at the door, shaking the students' hands, and saying a positive word or two to them as they left. Rollie tried to be last so he could linger with his favorite teacher. Not today. Today he was anxious to go to his room and find his marmalade jar. He hastily shook Mr. Chad's hand, and tried to squeeze away.

"Whoa there, horsey!" Mr. Chad tightened his grip on Rollie's hand. "Where are you off to in such a hurry?"

"Sorry, Mr. Chad, I've got a lot of work to do."

Mr. Chad studied Rollie's face. He leaned down and said in a low tone, "You're onto a mystery, aren't ya? I can see that spark in your eyes. Well, keep up the good work, Rollie. I could tell from the first day of class that you'd make a great detective."

Rollie's face lit up. He soaked up any compliment he could get, since it came rarely from his family. Not because they did not think he was great, but because they were always too consumed to notice. He relished this compliment now, especially since it came from someone he admired.

Straightening up, Mr. Chad hollered, "That's right, kid, we have class tomorrow, too. Now move along! Hello there, Miss Tibby."

Rollie raced upstairs, pushing past slowpokes along the stairs. He burst into his bedroom and dove under his bed. He pulled out one of his cardboard boxes and rummaged through it. He found the marmalade jar.

A good snack for the LIBRARY.

Rollie's instinct had been right about Auntie Ei: she knew more than she appeared to. He turned the jar up side down. His fingers traced an indentation in the bottom of the jar. A three. Rollie jumped to his feet and bumped into a friend.

"Cecily!"

"Rollie, I thought we were partners, but if you want to keep secrets, then go right ahead and keep your secrets." She turned on her heel and darted out before Rollie could respond.

He thought of going after her, but curiosity about his jar won in the end. He bounded downstairs and found the library empty and dark.

"Does anyone come in here?" he asked himself.

He made the room bright. He counted the third bookcase from the left, and inspected its side. Yep, a hole. He stuck his hand inside. Yep, a three. He turned his jar over in his hands until the three indentation was right side up like the raised three in the hole. He matched the end of the jar to the hole, and slid it in. A perfect fit. Even the threes matched. But the lip of the jar stuck out. Rollie pushed harder, but it would not go any further. Maybe that was the way it was supposed to fit. He was not sure what to do with the jar now, since nothing happened on its own. He tried to turn the jar to the left, but it would not budge. He turned to the right—

Click.

The jar turned and the bookcase swayed forward, as if on a hinge. Rollie peered behind the yawning bookcase. Through the shadows, he saw more bookshelves carved into the wall. Rows and rows of books crammed the shelves. He did not need to read each of their spines, for they all included the same two words in each of their somewhat varying titles: *Sherlock Holmes.*

"Our missing books!" Rollie gasped. He reached out his hand to grab one off the shelf—

"Hi, roomie!"

Rollie spun around to see Eliot enter the library. Rollie stepped in front of the open bookcase, slowly pushing it closed.

Click.

"Trying to solve the rearranging library, huh?" Eliot asked.

"Trying. What are you doing here?" His hands behind his back, Rollie slid the jar out of its hole.

Eliot plopped into an armchair. "I thought maybe I should try, too. I'm bored."

"Guess that's what you get for finishing your work so early in the morning." Rollie bit his lip. Probably not the nicest thing to say, but Eliot brought out the worst in him.

Eliot remained unaffected and shrugged. "I guess so. Want to go observe someone? Mr. Notch said it's good practice."

"I still have my work to do, remember?"

"Shame. See you at dinner."

"Okay." Rollie ducked out the door, hugging his jar and his thoughts to himself.

Later that night, he lay awake, trying to drown out Eliot and Rupert's snores with his own thoughts. So far, it was working, since Rollie had a lot to think about. Being alone with his thoughts also muddled his head. Finally he threw aside his covers, flicked on his flashlight, and found his hollow Shakespeare book on the desk. Inside he found his little notepad and pencil stub. He made a list of the Five Ws to record facts he knew so far, and questions he needed to find answers to.

WHO: Who else knows about the secret library?

WHAT: my marmalade jar is a key to a bookcase

WHERE: the secret shelves have our Sherlock Holmes

WHEN: Monday an attempted burglary in the library—related to secret in the library?

WHY: are our Holmes books hidden and why does the library rearrange if the real secret is behind?

Rollie chewed on the end of his pencil. He felt better after organizing his thoughts on paper. Before he flicked off his flashlight, he jotted down one more question.

P.S. What does Auntie Ei know?

Next morning, Rollie sat at a table on the rooftop, sipping his breakfast tea. His jar of marmalade stood next to his plate of hash browns. He had brought the jar with him, hoping to open the secret bookcase during recess. Cecily sat at another table with Tibby, trying to ignore him, but stealing occasional glances his way.

"Marmalade!" Eliot squealed. "Orange, right? That's my favorite! Can I have some for my toast, please?"

Rollie glanced nervously at Eliot, then at his jar. "I haven't taken the wax off yet."

"I know how to pop it off." Eliot gripped a butter knife.

Rollie slid the jar away from Eliot's reach. "I'd rather not share it. It's a gift from my great-aunt."

Eliot's face fell. "Sure, chum." He cast his eyes down to his plate.

Sighing, Rollie slid the jar across the table to Eliot. "Just a little won't hurt—but be careful with it."

"You're a great friend, you know that?" Eliot stabbed the wax with his butter knife, wriggled it around, and plucked out the wax plug. He spread a generous amount on his toast. "Just like home," he sighed with a mouthful.

"You eat marmalade at home?"

"Every morning. My nanny got me obsessed with it. She's the best ever. I miss her." Sadness crept into his eyes for a moment, but vanished when he took another bite of toast and marmalade.

"Where's your home?" Rollie asked him.

"Edinburgh."

"Scotland?" Rollie asked in surprise. "But you're English, aren't you?"

"My dad works there. My mum died, so I have my nanny. I don't get to go home until Christmas. It's too far for weekends."

"I'm sorry, Eliot."

"Don't be. It's the way life is. Making up rules about it doesn't change anything." Eliot finished his toast. "Perfect. Thanks for sharing."

"You can have as much as you want. I'll bring it to breakfast every morning."

"Really? Thanks! I should share something with you."

"You have. Your Sherlock Holmes comic books."

"Oh, yeah. Okay, we're even. I didn't really think about it, but I guess you kind of owed me that marmalade."

Rollie let the comment go—that was Eliot.

"Guess I'll go brush my teeth." Eliot stood, then sat back down. "Headmaster Yardsly and all the teachers. I forgot it's Tuesday."

Rollie craned his neck around to see the faculty parade out the rooftop door and over to the tables. On Tuesdays the faculty, including the headmaster, mingled among the students at breakfast time. Headmaster Yardsly thought it important to get to know all the students and make connections with them. Rollie had never known teachers to be so interested in and accessible to their students. It made him feel special.

Mr. Chadwick A. Permiter sauntered up to Rollie's table, standing between Rollie and Eliot. "Howdy, scholars! How do you feel about this Tuesday so far?"

"I think it will be a great Tuesday, Mr. Chad," Rollie replied.

"This marmalade has brightened my day!" Eliot exclaimed.

"Marmalade? Hmm…never cared for it much. Nothing beats my mom's strawberry-rhubarb jam."

"Rhubarb?" Rollie could not help making a face.

"I know, sounds gross, but with strawberries in jam, it's scrumptious. To each his own. See you boys later today." Mr. Chad gave them a thumbs-up signal and shuffled on to the next table.

Rollie's marmalade turned out to be the conversation topic of the morning. Every teacher commented about it when he or she stopped by to visit.

"Too sweet for my liking, although I am sure one could use the word in a code," Ms. Katherine E. Yardsly pointed out in her firm tone.

"Glass jars preserve wonderful prints!" Miss Amelia S. Hertz twittered, peering at the jar closely through her magnifying glass.

"Serving marmalade or any other type of spread directly from the jar is poor etiquette, you know," Professor Ichabod P. Enches muttered, his teeth clamped down on his pipe.

"I take a little marmalade with my afternoon toast every so often, I do," Mr. Percy E. Notch rambled, pushing his thick glasses up his nose.

"MARMALADE! Delectable stuff," Headmaster Sullivan P. Yardsly boomed.

Rollie watched each teacher closely in hopes of spotting a hint of recognition or knowing towards the marmalade jar. Either they excelled at hiding their thoughts, or they did not suspect that his jar was a key to the secret shelves. As the breakfast hour ended and the faculty returned indoors, Rollie cradled the jar in the crook of his arm and headed to class. Little did he know that his jar had indeed sparked the suspicion of one teacher.

CHAPTER 14

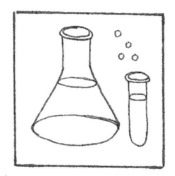

The First Hard Choice

Does anyone ever come in here?

Rollie found the answer to this question a frustrating *yes*. At recess, he had raced to the library only to find two upperclassmen studying for their history quiz. Books with the titles *Detectives in the Middle Ages* and *Roman Private Eyes* and *A Complete History of Spies from the Dark Ages* lay open in their laps.

At lunch, Rollie had wolfed down his sandwich and milk, much to the annoyance of Cecily, and had bounded to the library in hopes of finding it empty. Instead three first-year boys were there arguing about the rearranging library. After classes, he poked his head in and found Headmaster Yardsly and Ms. Yardsly engrossed in a hushed discussion. Rollie climbed upstairs, knowing he trailed behind in his independent studies and should probably spend the afternoon catching up. He fell asleep that night, annoyed.

But he dreamed.

He stood in his bedroom at home. All was quiet, until one by one his family and his teachers and even a few students like Rupert crowded into his room. They admired his telescope, his binoculars, his magnifying glass, and his book collection. Professor Enches said something about it being rude to spy on Mr. Crenshaw from the bedroom window. Then Ms. Yardsly jumped on the bed and bumped her head on the ceiling, which Rollie laughed at. Eliot came late and tried to squeeze into the room, but he could not fit and cried. Rollie felt bad for him. He looked around for Cecily, but she was not there. At one point, he heard a *clink* and saw a hand grab his marmalade jar, knock it against his bookshelf, and hide it under a handkerchief.

In the morning, Rollie smiled to himself, thinking how silly that dream was. He wished he could see Ms. Yardsly jump on a bed. He looked over at Eliot, asleep at the desk, his head on top of his books. Rollie felt a surprising warmth for him. Next, he wanted to find Cecily. Finally he reached out for his marmalade jar, but—

"It's gone!"

He buzzed around the room, checking under all three beds and atop the desk cluttered with books and Eliot. He stopped in the center of the tiny room, turning around, looking every which way. He shook Eliot's shoulder.

"The square root of forty-nine is seven!"

"Eliot, wake up!"

"I wasn't asleep!" Eliot snapped, threatening with a grumpy glare.

"Did you take my marmalade jar?"

Eliot stretched and yawned. "No, but marmalade does sound yummy right now!"

"It's gone."

"What? Where to?"

"I don't know. I had it here with me last night, and when I woke up this morning it was gone."

"Odd, and a pity. I was looking forward to having some with my toast this morning." Eliot closed his books, and pulled on a sweater. "Don't worry about it."

"I should tell Headmaster Yardsly."

"Honestly, Rollie, it's just a jar of marmalade."

It's not just a jar of marmalade.

Rollie sprinted out the door, through the hall, and down the stairs. He did not want to assume too much too soon, but he had an instinct that someone purposely stole his jar, knowing its true value, knowing it was more than just a jar of marmalade. Rollie's detective mind steamed into full gear.

Who would take it?

The answer did not come easily to him. He tried another question.

Who knew he had it?

That second answer jolted him with a sinking feeling: *practically everyone knew he had it.* Yesterday morning at breakfast every teacher had commented on it, lots of students had seen it, and his roommate had enjoyed it. Too many suspects.

Why had someone stolen it?

That answer did not lend new insight: *obviously to open the secret library.* The culprit would not be a teacher, since the teachers probably all knew how to open the secret library...or did they? Well, at least Rollie's first hunch had been right: the secret library held importance.

By now the school day had started as more students emerged from their rooms and made their way up to the roof for breakfast. Some gave Rollie confused looks as he pushed past them in the opposite direction—downstairs. He reached Headmaster Yardsly's office on the bottom floor. Taking a deep breath, he lightly rapped on the door.

"ENTER!"

Rollie turned the knob slowly, and pushed in the door. His eyes glimmered as they took in the office. A fireplace and bearskin rug stole the focus of the room. Two cozy armchairs squatted before it. A mantel clock *tick-tocked* quietly. Several holes initialing V.R. riddled the mantel; Rollie knew revolver bullets had carved those holes a long time ago. A penknife stabbed notes to the mantel. Bookshelves, crammed with books, flanked either side of the fireplace. Rollie remembered Holmes' disorderly method of recording his cases. To the right against a window loomed a large messy desk. Rollie's eyes roamed around the room to the right corner nearest the door. A homemade chemistry lab hoarded that corner, complete with beakers, test tubes, and microscope. To his left hung heavy draperies, which Rollie knew concealed a private sitting area. A few items decorated the walls: a violin and bow, an unframed portrait of Henry Ward Beecher, and a photograph of Irene Adler, the only woman to ever best Holmes. Lastly, Rollie recognized a black silhouette of a man with a hawk-shaped nose and prominent forehead.

As Rollie stepped into the homey room, he felt as if he stepped into another world, a fictional world. He had only read about this room, its décor and items, yet he knew it as well as his own bedroom.

"Those are the bullet holes that Holmes made when he practiced shooting his revolver," Rollie said excitedly, pointing to the mantel. "And that's his lab where he studied evidence. Is that really his violin?"

Headmaster Yardsly smiled as he stood behind his desk, his lean figure outlined against the window. "It is. Have you not been in here before?"

Rollie shook his head. "I would have visited sooner if I knew your office was Holmes' actual flat. *The* 221b."

"Well, then WELCOME!" the headmaster boomed as usual. "Why are you visiting me this morning?" He sat back down as Rollie approached the desk.

With great effort, Rollie dragged his eyes from his surroundings and focused on his headmaster. "Something of mine has been stolen, sir."

Yardsly's eyebrows shot up. "From your room?"

"Yes, sir, last night. When I woke up this morning, it was gone. I can't find it anywhere. I know I had it right next to me last night when—"

"HOLD ON!" Yardsly raised his long hand. Back to a normal pitch, he inquired, "What exactly was stolen?"

"My marmalade jar, sir." Rollie watched the headmaster's reaction closely.

Yardsly's keen eyes narrowed slightly as he studied his student. The mantel clock *tick-tocked*, being the only noise in the room for a good five seconds. "Where did the jar come from?"

"Home, sir. My Auntie Ei gave it to me."

At the mention of that name, Yardsly's eyes widened slightly. "Why did your aunt give you a—"

"My great-aunt."

"Why did your GREAT-AUNT give you a jar of marmalade? Seems a very odd gift."

"She said it would be a good snack to enjoy in the *library*," Rollie emphasized the last word.

"Did she? Have you used—I mean, enjoyed it in the library yet?"

"I tried to yesterday, sir, but there was someone always in there. I know why she suggested the library."

Another uneasy five seconds *ticked* by, the headmaster and the student regarding one another. Finally Yardsly told him, "Step closer, Rollin. No, closer. That's good. Listen carefully: students are not permitted to have marmalade jars in the library. Teachers aren't, either. Of course stealing is wrong and normally I would address the student body about it. That usually forces the culprit to light. However, a stolen marmalade jar is a dangerous thing. I myself keep mine hidden. So until I can investigate this, it's best to keep it a secret. Understand?"

Rollie nodded, understanding perfectly what Headmaster Yardsly meant. They both knew the significance of the jar, but refrained from admitting it openly.

"You're a good boy, Rollin, and a fine student, so I hear. You did the right thing coming to me. Now get to breakfast before you miss it."

Rollie turned to go, but stopped and asked, "Does my stolen jar have anything to do with that burglary?"

Headmaster Yardsly rubbed his square chin in thought. "Possibly. You're a fine sleuth. Do you have any other similar jars?"

"No, sir, just the one."

Yardsly nodded. "Happy Wednesday to you then!"

Smiling, Rollie slipped out the office and raced upstairs to breakfast. He barely gobbled down his hash browns when the bell rang. Taking one last swig of tea, he hurried off to class. He had a hard time focusing in class because his mind tingled with questions, faces, and guesses.

In Ms. Yardsly's Decoding Course Level One, Rollie jotted down a list of everyone he knew for sure had seen his marmalade jar yesterday. To be safe, he wrote it all in code. He had learned his lesson about leaving things out in the open, even things as trivial-seeming as marmalade jars. At the bottom of the list he added *unknown thief.*

During recess, Rollie searched his room one more time just to be sure it really was gone. He found no trace of the jar.

Rollie was glad Miss Hertz did not make them work in pairs today to analyze prints like she usually did in her Identification of Fingerprint, Footprint, and Ash class. Instead she had them silently read a monograph written by Sherlock Holmes himself titled *The Tracing of Footsteps*. This gave Rollie more time to mull over his case. He decided during lunch he would search his room for any "teeny but mighty evidence", as Miss Hertz referred to prints and dust.

As Professor Enches droned on and on about the proper decorum between a private eye and a member of Scotland Yard in his Spy Etiquette and Interrogation class, Rollie came up with a plan to *politely* interrogate a few classmates who had sat with him the other morning and had seen his jar.

Rollie ate lunch in his room. Munching on his sandwich, Rollie used his magnifying glass to inspect the room. He inspected the door, the doorframe, and the floor. Either he was not as good of a detective as he had hoped, or the burglar was very careful, for he found nothing helpful.

While Mr. Notch acted out a scenario for the students to observe in his Observation class, Rollie thought about doing a little observation of his own. He realized whoever had stolen his jar would want to use it soon. Last time, the burglar had broken into the library during the night. Rollie made plans to hide out in the library that night, in hopes of catching the burglar. The idea fluttered in his middle.

Normally Rollie anticipated his last class of the day with Mr. Chad, but today he could not concentrate in the Disguise class. He pondered the idea of wearing a disguise of some sort. He did not really have anything…

"Listen, sleuths, you don't need to own a costume shop to disguise yourself. Your own wardrobe holds a lot of disguises. You just have to know how to apply them. Holmes fooled everyone with his disguises because he didn't just wear the part, he *became* the part. He used common clothes and items. So think twice before you throw away that hideous sweater with an embroidered yak that your great-aunt Bertha gave you for Christmas."

In the end, Rollie decided to wear black. After class, Rollie met Cecily on his way upstairs.

"Hi, Cecily."

She kept her eyes ahead and said nothing.

"How's your day been?"

Silent as a grave, Rollie thought.

"Why are you mad at me?"

"If you don't know, then I can't help you," Cecily retorted.

Rollie rolled his eyes. He had heard his mother say that to his father a few times, always when they were in a bit of a fight. It did not happen very often, but he remembered that expression because it seemed ridiculous.

"I've been busy, Cecily. Sorry I haven't been around much."

"Exactly. Busy with what?" She stopped on the stairs and faced him with a stern glare.

Digging his hands into his pockets, Rollie wondered what to say. He wanted to tell her all about the mystery, but he knew Headmaster Yardsly would not want him to. Yet Cecily was his friend, his sleuthing partner. On the other hand, he remembered how Holmes had always kept things from Watson. Whenever he read that, he felt bad for Watson and disliked Holmes' arrogance in keeping all facts to himself. Rollie thought if he had kept more things secret, he would still have his marmalade jar. He sighed and made his choice on how to answer her.

"Busy with schoolwork."

Cecily eyed him. Rollie could tell she knew he was lying, and he saw the hurt in her eyes. Without another word, she took off upstairs.

Rollie knew he had made the wrong choice.

CHAPTER 15

The Betrayal

"*I* got you something," Eliot beamed as Rollie entered their room after dinner.

"You did? That's nice."

Eliot held something behind his back. "Guess."

"Is it something for school?"

"No. Well… kind of. Actually, no."

"Okay… Is it something for fun?"

"Um…you could use it for fun, but not really, so no."

"What is it?"

"Give up? Because once you give up I win. That's the rule."

"Sure, I give up."

Eliot held out a sealed jar of orange marmalade. "Here. I noticed you were sad about losing your other one. Plus I really need marmalade on my toast."

Rollie was about to ask why Eliot did not buy himself a jar, but he knew he should say something different. "Thank you, Eliot. That's really kind of you."

"What are friends for?" Eliot shrugged.

Smiling, Rollie agreed. "Yeah, you're a nice friend."

"I don't have nice friends," a voice from the doorway interrupted.

Both boys turned to see Rupert. He wore his usual glum expression on his round face. He plopped onto his bed.

"Do you have *any* friends?" Rollie ventured to ask.

"Of course I do! What a rude question. They're just not *nice* friends."

"Then they aren't really friends," Eliot argued. "That's a rule of friendship—friends should treat each other nicely, otherwise it does no good to keep them."

"That is a good rule," Rollie admitted, thinking it was the first good rule Eliot had come up with. "We'll be your friends, Rupert."

"No thank you." With that, Rupert rolled over on his side and fell asleep.

CHAPTER FIFTEEN

*   *   *   *

Rollie turned the doorknob. He paused, gripping the knob in his sweaty palm before leaning the door open.

Squeak, the door warned quietly.

He stepped into the room and glanced around quickly. The library was cold and gloomy. A pale glow from the street lamp outside illuminated one corner of the library. The light seeped through the one good window. The other window that had been broken was still covered with a board. Rollie joined the center of the library, pondering his hiding place.

The library did not lend itself to good hiding places. There was a decent hiding spot between the armchairs and end table, but that was too near the window. Rollie figured the burglar would enter through a window like before. The only other hiding places were in between the bookcases, where Rollie could easily fit. But the bookcases were the burglar's targets. He had no other choice. Rollie crouched between the bookcases closest to the door, to be near his escape in case he was discovered. From here he could see the windows and the bookcase that opened with his marmalade jar. That bookcase would be the burglar's first stop. Snug in his hiding place, Rollie tried to calm his breathing.

Inhale, exhale, inhale, exhale.

As much as he tried, he could not slow his racing heartbeat or the insistent flutter in his stomach. He patted his moist palms on his thighs, then wrapped his arms around his knees and hugged them. The last he checked, Eliot's clock read twelve-ten. Rollie guessed it had to be around twelve-twenty now. He hoped the burglar would not be too late…if he was coming at all…

As the minutes crawled by, Rollie's thoughts trickled into each other, leading him through a mind maze. He remembered one Christmas Eve, when he was younger, he could not fall asleep, so he let his mind wander. Often he retraced his thoughts to exercise his deductive reasoning skill because Holmes argued the ability to reason backwards was invaluable to solving a case. When Rollie retraced his thoughts, he laughed at the way they linked together.

They linked like a chain…just like the chain securing a black box to a lamppost down the road from his house. Last winter he and Cecily had discovered it, and had thought it was the strangest mystery to their neighborhood in a long time. When they asked Mr. Wilson about it, he told them the lamppost had broken, and the contents of that box temporarily kept the lamp operating. Rollie and Cecily had been quite disappointed. It had appeared to be very intriguing, but turned out to be very boring.

In the same way, someone had appeared to be one thing, but had turned out to be a thief, stealing Rollie's jar. Who? Surely a person here at school, which meant it was someone appearing to be someone different. A chill prickled up Rollie's spine. As much as he wanted to see who the burglar was, he was hesitant to know the truth. He shook his head clear of thoughts. Being a detective meant finding the truth…at all costs…

Squeak.

Rollie's ears perked up, his heartbeat escalated, and his breathing quickened. He squinted through the gloom at the windows—nothing there. His eyes darted towards the door—it opened!

So far Rollie's assumptions held true that the burglar was in the school, entering like a typical member. The burglar must have broken the library window the first time to give the false idea it was an outside job. Rollie did not recognize the person's face, for it was hidden in shadow beneath a cap. But he did recognize the adult's clothing— his heart nearly stopped. The flutter hardened into a pit in his stomach. And a new element plagued him: pain.

The intruder wore a cap and a dreary coat with an upturned collar. From the glow of the street lamp, Rollie could see a red cravat around his neck.

"By the way, the fun thing about a disguise like that one is that you can be any type of worker and loafer."

As his face heated, Rollie remembered the words of his beloved teacher. As much as he wished it to be untrue, the truth fleshed out before him: the burglar appeared to be Mr. Chad in his loafer disguise.

Rollie watched him cross the room to a bookcase, a marmalade jar clutched in his hand. The *loafer* fit the marmalade jar in the bookcase's hole, turned the jar, and opened the bookcase. A beam from a flashlight flicked on. With this light, Rollie could see the contents of the secret bookcase. Shelves and shelves of Sherlock Holmes books lined the interior. The intruder grabbed one book and thumbed through it. Unsatisfied, he slid it back into place and grabbed another one. After a few looks through a few books, the burglar found what he wanted and tucked the book under his arm.

Click, he pushed the bookcase closed and headed for the door.

He stopped.

He turned.

He stared in Rollie's direction.

Rollie froze.

The burglar turned back to the door and slunk out of the library.

Rollie could not move. He huddled in his hiding place, clenching his fists. He wanted to let his thoughts wander, but they would not; they focused on one thing: Mr. Chad the burglar. He felt stunned at the truth he had just witnessed. Why did it have to be Mr. Chad, his favorite teacher? *How* could it be Mr. Chad, such a fun and likeable person?

Beware of him, echoed Auntie Ei's words in his head.

Rollie clenched tighter. *She* had given him the marmalade jar. *She* had warned him about Mr. Chad. What did Auntie Ei really know? As much as Rollie wanted to funnel blame on his great-aunt, he knew in his heart he had to face the real culprit, his teacher.

With a shaky breath, Rollie stumbled to his feet and quitted the library. He wearily climbed the three flights of stairs back to his floor. With each heavy step, his mind tossed between two choices: turn in Mr.

Chad or ignore the situation and wait for someone else to catch him. Surely the law or Headmaster Yardsly would solve the mystery if Rollie could. Rollie did not think he had the strength to report Mr. Chad. Tears stung his eyes as he thought about no more classes with Mr. Chad. Headmaster would hire another teacher for the class. A pity; there was no one as fun.

It was not just fun that made Mr. Chad his favorite teacher. Rollie remembered how Mr. Chad had recognized Rollie's detecting skills and had complimented him, saying he had noticed what a fine detective Rollie would make. Had that been a lie too? Rollie had never felt a betrayal before, believing someone to be a certain way, only to discover it was all a lie.

It hurt.

He crept into bed, pulled the covers up to his chin, and closed his eyes. At first he could not fall asleep, but the night's events had taken toll on him. He soon drifted off.

He did not dream.

CHAPTER 16

The Second Hard Choice

"*W*ake up, sleepy head!" Eliot sang as he pounced on Rollie.

Grumbling, Rollie hid under the covers.

"You're going to miss breakfast. Either way I'm taking that marmalade with me."

"I don't want marmalade. I'm sick of it."

Eliot gasped. "How on earth can you say such a thing? You're not in your right mind. Get up!" He yanked the covers off Rollie.

For a moment, Rollie smiled. Then last night's events replayed in his mind, and he frowned. Instead of a flutter, he felt a pain. He fought back tears.

"What's the matter with you?" Eliot peered closely at Rollie's blood-shot eyes. "Are you sick? If you're sick, go home. I do *not* want to get sick."

"I'm not sick." Rollie started to undress.

"Why are you wearing all black?"

Rollie grimaced. He forgot what he was wearing. "It's the only thing clean right now. I got to take laundry home this weekend."

"Or you need to pack more. See you upstairs." Eliot bustled out of the room, taking the jar of marmalade.

Rollie pulled on his trousers and a gray shirt. His hair stuck out every which way, but he did not care. He trudged upstairs to the roof. He took one look at the students eating and chatting and giggling, then turned and went back downstairs. His appetite for food and conversation were gone. Back in his room, he threw himself on his bed and stared up at the ceiling. Alone with his thoughts, he came to a decision: he would not turn Mr. Chad in, not yet anyway. Right now he could not bear to do it. He would mull it over during the weekend and start anew on Monday.

Yep, that was what he would do.

*   *   *   *

The rest of the day Rollie felt detached, absent from reality. He attended his classes, took notes, smiled politely at his teachers, and shuffled down the halls with his classmates. No one bothered him; he talked to no one.

He dreaded attending Disguising class, and almost ditched, but did not want to raise suspicion. As he watched Mr. Chad be his usual boisterous and humorous self, Rollie knew this was just another disguise the teacher donned. He found it hard to believe that behind the attractive exterior, Mr. Chad was a villain. For the first time, Rollie was afraid. He shivered. After class, Rollie navigated to avoid Mr. Chad, hoping not to be stopped at the door. No such luck.

"Rollie, you look awful! You okay?"

His eyes cast down, Rollie nodded. He started perspiring.

"Yeah right! What's wrong? You can tell me."

Rollie swallowed, his heartbeat quickening. "I'm just a little homesick."

"Don't be embarrassed about that. Even I get homesick. You know what I miss most right now? Pizza! There's this fabulous Italian cafe right down the street from my folks. It makes *the* best—"

"Sorry, I need to go." Rollie pulled away, hoping Mr. Chad could not read the terror in his eyes.

*　　　　*　　　　*　　　　*

Friday afternoon finally came. Rollie wanted nothing more than to retreat home and surround himself with his crazy yet comforting family. He also had a thing or two to ask Auntie Ei. He was a tad disappointed and a bit relieved when the cab driver told him Cecily had taken a separate hansom home. Rollie had to fix things between Cecily and him, but first he had to rid himself of the current awful truth. Although he decided not to turn in Mr. Chad, he did not feel any better.

Did he feel badly due to the situation, or because he made the wrong choice to do nothing? He needed more time to digest it, hence the weekend home.

When Rollie got home at sunset, he found the house quiet and nearly empty. His brothers were still at work, his mother had taken his sisters into town for new shoes, and his father was working late at the university. Rollie abandoned his suitcase full of dirty laundry in the entry hall and headed for his bedroom.

"Sick of stairs," he mumbled as he climbed and climbed. He passed Auntie Ei's bedroom, looking back over his shoulder into her open doorway.

"Hello, Rollin," her voice croaked from inside.

Rollie edged into her room. "Hello, Auntie Ei. How are you?"

"Old, of course. How are you?"

"Alright, I guess."

Auntie Ei flashed her eyes from her book to Rollie. "If you are alright, then I am a little girl again."

Rollie could not help smiling at her silly comment. Then he frowned, knowing the confrontation that needed to come. "Auntie Ei, why did you give me that marmalade jar? Did you know what it was for? Where did you get it?"

"Young man, that is an inexcusable number of questions for someone so old as me to answer. I daresay you are upset."

Rollie took a deep breath to calm himself. Straining to keep his voice low, he asked again, "Why did you give it to me?"

"A good question," Auntie Ei approved. "I gave it to you to use. How did you use it?"

"I used it to open the secret library."

"There you have it. I'm afraid there's nothing more mysterious about it," the old woman said very matter-of-factly.

"Yes, there is, Auntie," Rollie countered, surprised at his own assertiveness. "How did you get that jar? Headmaster Yardsly is the only person I know who has one."

"If you must know, I am an active member on the Sherlock Academy Board of Trustees."

"You are?" This answered his suspicion about her connection to the school. "So it's okay that you have one?"

"There is nothing illegal about having a marmalade jar, Rollin."

"Headmaster Yardsly said those jars are dangerous."

"In the hands of the wrong people, they are. You and I are not *wrong people*."

Tears misted his eyes as he thought about who the *wrong people*, or wrong *person*, were. "Auntie, if someone knows the truth…and that someone doesn't say anything about it…"

"Go on, Rollin."

"Then is that the same as lying?"

Auntie Ei studied him before answering. "I suppose so."

"And that's wrong, right?"

"I haven't the slightest idea why you're asking me. You're an intelligent boy. You ought to know the difference between right and wrong."

Rollie nodded. "It's hard doing the right thing sometimes."

"Almost always. That's what makes it the right thing. We naturally want to do the wrong thing most of the time."

"Why?"

"The discussion of right versus wrong is a very tedious one, and I don't believe I will live much longer to endure that. Perhaps there's an easier discussion we can engage in."

"I know something about someone. I don't want to say anything about him because I really like him. I want someone else to expose him."

"It sounds very vague, but I respect your privacy. Let me ask you this: you are a detective, correct?"

"Yes, at least I hope so."

"Rollin, you know very well that you are, and a good one at that. Stop trying to sound modest in this instance, for it comes off as insecurity. There is a difference between being modest and being insecure. You must be confident in who you are without being arrogant—that's modesty. Next question: what does a detective do?"

"I know what a detective—"

"Answer the question, Rollin Edgar Wilson."

"A detective follows clues to solve a mystery and find out who is guilty."

Auntie Ei pointed a bony finger at him. "There you have it. A detective finds who is guilty and brings that person to justice. Would a detective be doing his job if he discovered the guilty person but never reported him?"

Rollie shook his head.

"That detective might as well retire and become a bee-keeper! A detective always chooses to do the right thing at any cost; otherwise no one would employ him. Holmes believed that everyone was responsible for preserving justice." Auntie Ei dropped her eyes down to her book.

Rollie backed into the broad hallway. He made it up to his room and sat at his desk by the window overlooking Mr. Crenshaw's garden. Mr. Crenshaw was not there—a good thing since Rollie did not feel like spying on him. Instead he looked around at his telescope, his magnifying glass, his notes tacked on the cork-covered wall, and his collection of Sherlock Holmes books. He thought about Auntie Ei's advice.

And he knew what he had to do.

CHAPTER 17

Double Flutters

*A*s the weekend wore on, Rollie felt better. Being around his family gave him the comfort he needed. Usually he got annoyed with dinnertime, but this weekend he relished it, realizing he missed their interruptions and their teasing. He even felt better about the situation at school. Still something was not quite right.

Cecily.

He called on her Saturday, but found her not at home. He tried again Sunday afternoon. At first she did not want to see him, but when he persisted at the front door, she reluctantly met him on the porch. They sat together on the front porch steps.

"What do you want? I'm right in the middle of homework."

"Homework?" Rollie raised his eyebrows. "We don't have homework."

Cecily blushed. In a small voice, she confessed, "I didn't finish my independent studies for the week."

"I didn't know you could take unfinished work home."

"I'm not sure you can. I'm being sneaky about it."

Rollie gave her a look of disapproval.

"I'll talk to Headmaster about it first thing Monday morning."

"Guess we'll both be bothering him first thing Monday morning."

"What do you have to talk to him about?"

"That's why I came over here. I need to tell you what I've been up to."

"About time. Go ahead."

Rollie recounted the week's discoveries. Cecily's eyes widened when he told her his marmalade jar was the library key and it had been stolen. Her mouth dropped open when he concluded that Mr. Chad was the culprit.

"That makes me sad," she sighed. "I really like him."

"So do I. He's my favorite teacher."

"I suppose he won't be teaching anymore."

"Probably. It's been hard for me, but I know the right thing to do is turn him in. I should have told you about this. Sorry."

Cecily smiled. "No harm done. I mean, besides hurting my feelings for a little bit. You know, for as much as I love Holmes, I never liked how he left Watson out of the loop. I felt like Watson this week."

"Well, I'm not Holmes and you're not Watson. I'm Rollie and you're my best friend Cecily. That's all that matters." Rollie socked her shoulder playfully.

When Rollie got home from visiting Cecily, he found a letter on the hall table addressed to Professor Enches. He grimaced.

"Mum!" he called, finding his way to his mother's workroom. Mrs. Wilson had a room in the back of the house full of projects that kept her busy, like mending, quilting, and occasionally sketching when she found the time. Usually on Sundays she worked on her charcoal sketches.

"What is it, my Rollie?"

"This letter for Professor Enches. Am I to deliver it?"

"Yes, on Monday. It's from Mr. Crenshaw. That's awfully nice of you to deliver his letters for him. I'm sure it saves a great deal of postage for him." Mrs. Wilson wiped her blackened thumb on her cloth.

"I guess," Rollie muttered, leaving his mother to sketch. Rollie stood in the hallway, eyeing the envelope in his hands. It was sealed. He held it up to the sunlight glittering through a nearby hall window. The stationary was too thick to reveal writing. Curiosity gnawed at Rollie;

he wanted to read what was inside. He almost ripped it open, but shook his head. Nope, that was definitely not the right thing to do.

At dinner that night, the family conversation bantered away as usual.

"Fact: another week is upon us," Mr. Wilson began.

"Alice is leaving town," Stewart whined, gnawing on his drumstick.

"The family's been warned! Stew will be moping around for the next week," Edward joked.

"Why is Alice leaving town?" Mrs. Wilson asked, passing Daphne the rolls.

"Holiday with her folks."

"Daddy," Lucille piped up. "When can we go on holiday?"

"We just went on holiday in June."

"That was a long time ago!"

"Fact: two months is not a long time ago, darling."

"To me it is."

"Let's talk about this week," said Mr. Wilson, changing the subject. "Fact: this is my last week of working until lunchtime. September is fast upon us. What else is happening this week?"

"My quilting group," Mrs. Wilson replied. "I'm hosting it here. Does everyone hear that? The parlor will be occupied by women this Thursday afternoon from two to four."

"Do we have violin lessons, mummy?" Daphne asked.

"Yes, on Tuesday."

Daphne and Lucille groaned in unison.

"Stop, girls, violin lessons are good for you. Rollie liked them, didn't you?"

Rollie shrugged. "They were okay."

"Oh, Rollie, what will you be doing this week?" Mr. Wilson questioned.

"Doing the right thing," Auntie Ei cut in, nodding knowingly at Rollie.

"Auntie's right, Dad."

"That's good to hear. Fact: doing the right thing always pays off." Mr. Wilson raised his glass to toast this wise saying.

*   *   *   *

"Are you ready then?" Cecily asked Monday morning as she and Rollie bumped along in their horse-drawn cab.

"Yes, I am," Rollie said resolutely. "It's the right thing to do."

The hansom pulled up to 221 Baker Street. Rollie and Cecily hopped out and waved to their cab driver. They mounted the porch steps and entered the school. It was relatively quiet—a difference from last Monday morning when they had arrived at a crime scene. Embarking upon their third week at the academy, they felt at home as they stood in the entry hall. Both children stepped up to the headmaster's door and knocked together.

No answer.

Knock-knock!

No answer.

They opened the door a crack and peeked inside. All was dark.

"Headmaster Yardsly is on an errand!"

Rollie jumped; Cecily squealed. Both turned around to find themselves a little too close to Ms. Yardsly. She stood tall with her hands behind her back. Her hair twisted into its tight bun. Her brown suit looked crisper than ever, as did her expression.

"Do you know when he'll be back, Ms. Yardsly?" Rollie ventured to ask.

"He should return in the next few hours. Get to breakfast immediately. Tardiness is not tolerated." She narrowed her eyes and watched them scamper upstairs.

When they got to the fourth floor, Rollie and Cecily stopped to catch their breath.

"She can be so scary!" Cecily giggled.

"Bad luck Headmaster being out. I'm sick of carrying this secret around. I want to get it out, over, and done with."

"What secret?" a new voice cut in.

Rollie saw Eliot coming towards them down the hall.

"Hey, Eliot, how was your weekend?"

"What secret?"

"If I told you, it wouldn't be a secret."

"Cecily knows," Eliot argued.

"It's just a secret between us."

Eliot's face betrayed hurt feelings.

Cecily jumped in. "Actually, Eliot, it's about my parents. They're not getting along right now. I'm a little sensitive about it."

Eliot's face softened. "Sorry, Cecily. That's too bad. I won't pry."

"Thank you, Eliot. Breakfast?"

The three students headed up to the roof for breakfast. When Eliot got lost in the crowd, Rollie leaned into Cecily and whispered, "Thanks for that, but you didn't have to lie for me."

"I didn't lie. I told the truth."

Rollie frowned. "I'm sorry. I didn't know that—"

"Never mind. I guess that's why I was a little more sensitive this week than usual."

"You should have told me."

"Let's take care of one problem at a time. If you meet with Headmaster, let me know how it goes."

Rollie gulped. "I will." He felt the weight of his task burden his heart. Sticking his hands into his pockets, he felt the envelope for Professor Enches. He was tired of carrying that around, too. Forgetting breakfast, he ran downstairs to leave it on Professor Enches' desk. One less thing to worry about.

He found the classroom empty and dark. He flicked on the light and padded between the desks and chairs. Professor Enches' desk was tidy as ever. Rollie placed the envelope in the center of the desk, facing the professor's chair so he would see it as soon as he sat down. Rollie turned to leave, but stopped when something caught his eye. Something red and frayed peeked out from underneath the desk.

Rollie stooped for a closer look. He reached out his fingertips and grabbed it.

A red cravat.

In one second, Rollie felt a flutter of sickish surprise and a flutter of welcomed relief. He knew right away it was Mr. Chad's disguise, but what was it doing under Professor Enches' desk? Clearly this indicated that Professor Enches was the disguised culprit Rollie had seen in the library. Rollie felt relieved. Or did Mr. Chad stash it under the professor's desk to pass the blame on him? Rollie felt queasy again. He hoped the first indication was the truth, that the professor had used Mr. Chad's disguise. Rollie needed more evidence to affirm his conclusion. Holmes always warned against relying on circumstantial evidence, and impressed the importance of details. Was there a detail Rollie missed?

The letter.

Stuffing the red cravat back under the desk, Rollie reached for the letter. Yesterday curiosity had almost compelled him to open the letter, but today desperation drove him to tear it open. He stood with his back to the door, so did not notice someone enter the room as he tore a corner of the envelope.

"Good morning, Rollin E. Wilson."

CHAPTER 18

A New Hat

Rollie jumped and reflexively stuffed the letter under his shirt—the quickest hiding place he could think of. When he spun around, he was face to face with Professor Enches. The professor clasped his hands behind his back, puffed on his pipe, and eyed the boy closely.

"What brings you to my classroom this early in the morning?" he asked in a low tone.

"I, uh, was just delivering a letter." With a shaky hand, Rollie took the envelope out from under his shirt and held it out to the professor.

Professor Enches stared at it. "Why is the corner torn?"

"Sorry, sir, it, uh, got a bit torn in my pocket. I was just about to leave it on your desk like you asked me to."

Professor Enches blocked Rollie's path of escape. Rollie swallowed and blinked. The professor stared at him. Rollie kept wondering, *Does he know that I know?* Although Rollie had no reason to feel guilty, he felt his stomach churning. Finally, Professor Enches took the letter and stepped aside to let Rollie exit. Once through the door, Rollie ran downstairs, not stopping until he reached the headmaster's office. Panting outside the door, he rapped on it, hoping the headmaster was back.

No luck.

Rollie swallowed. After that encounter, he felt sure Professor Enches was the culprit; yet Rollie did not want to be a detective who acted on feelings. Still he had an instinct. Auntie Ei had encouraged him to act on his instincts. So far his instincts had served him well, but he knew he also needed evidence. Maybe it was good Headmaster Yardsly was not back yet. Rollie needed to build his case a little stronger. His instinct told him the key was in those letters.

Getting a letter would be tricky.

He needed help.

He needed his Watson.

By eleven-thirty, the plan was set. Rollie filed into the room with his classmates. He took his usual seat. Professor Enches stood from his desk and began his lecture. Rollie appeared to be listening intently, keeping his eyes on the professor, jotting down a few notes here and there. Everything seemed normal, except Cecily's chair stood vacant. It took all Rollie's concentration to appear normal and attentive, but inside he was a mess of flutter. Just when he thought he would give away the whole plan, the classroom door creaked open and Cecily's head popped in.

"Excuse me, professor," Cecily called in a little voice.

"Excuse *me*," Professor Enches huffed in an agitated tone.

"May I please speak with you for just a moment, sir?" Cecily requested in her most polite way. "It's extremely important to me." She looked like she might cry, so the professor marched over to her.

All the students turned their heads to see the disturbance. That was exactly what Rollie hoped for. In a blink, he was behind the professor's desk, opening drawers, searching for a letter.

"I'm very upset about this…right now…and I just—" Cecily burst into loud wails.

"There, there, now, tears are no proper display of etiquette."

Frantically, Rollie shuffled through the desk drawers. He slid them closed just as he noticed the professor's briefcase on the floor—a thick parchment envelope stuck out. Rollie snatched it and stuffed it under his shirt as one scrawny boy in the front spotted him. The boy gaped, mouth ajar. Rollie put his finger to his lips, signaling the boy to remain silent.

But the boy was just like Rollie, and thought it his duty to report any crimes.

"Professor Enches!"

The professor spun around as Rollie reached his seat.

"Professor Enches! He was behind your desk!" the little boy announced, pointing an accusing finger at Rollie.

Rollie paled as the professor marched over to him.

"Rollin E. Wilson, you have gone too far. No student is allowed behind a teacher's desk." He glared at Rollie, his mustache twitching. Abruptly, he barked, "Class dismissed!"

Murmurs of confusion stirred.

"This instant!" the professor shouted.

Students scrambled out of their seats and pushed through the door. Rollie ventured after them, but got caught by Enches' hand. Cecily cast him a terrified expression as she was herded out by her peers. The door slammed shut.

Professor Enches gripped Rollie's collar, yanked him over to a nearby chair, and pushed him into it. He eyed Rollie closely, searching his face. Enches' flushed complexion faded and his breathing slowed as he regained his composure.

Rollie sat very still, as if any sudden movement might trigger the professor's temper. He also did not want to betray the envelope beneath his shirt. Seconds dragged into minutes as the teacher and student silently regarded one another. Finally one of them initiated the inevitable.

"Why were you behind my desk?"

Rollie gulped.

"It's bad etiquette to not answer your elders."

"I have my reasons, sir," Rollie managed with more courage than he thought he had.

"You are a bright lad, but I am smarter still. I know what you were after."

Rollie tried to read the professor's expression. Was he bluffing in hopes of Rollie confessing? Or did he suspect Rollie of knowing the truth? Rollie mustered more courage and tried to bait back.

"Sir, why don't you report me to Headmaster?"

Professor Enches' mustache twitched again. "I do not wish to inconvenience Headmaster. I'm sure you and I can resolve this properly."

He knows that I know, Rollie realized with dread. His only safety was the headmaster. If he could convince Enches to turn him in—

"Listen, lad, I do not want us to be enemies. If you confess, I will spare you punishment. I recognize great character in you, that is the reason I chose you to deliver my letters."

Rollie found himself believing the professor, believing in the sincerity and the high regard Enches had for him. Maybe he had assumed too quickly that Enches was the guilty player in this mystery. Perhaps he should hand over the letter...

"Be wise and tell me the truth," Enches coaxed.

No. Whether the letter incriminated or exonerated Enches, it was too valuable to give up. Rollie would not possess evidence like this again. He had to keep it, and he had to get it to Headmaster Yardsly…at all costs.

Rollie's demeanor changed. His jaw clenched firmly, his gaze hardened, and his body stiffened with resolution. The professor noticed.

With shocking speed, Enches lunged forward and pinned Rollie's arms to his sides with an iron grip. He pushed his face forward, inches from Rollie's. Rollie could feel hot breath against his cheeks. The professor's polite façade melted away with his villainous temper.

In a vehement whisper, Enches threatened, "You are no match for us. You have no idea who you are dealing with. You *will* cooperate."

Rollie trembled, but bravely held his teacher's gaze. Rollie's arms tingled as if they were falling asleep, so tight was Enches' grip.

Knock-knock!

Both teacher and pupil jumped with alarm. The professor released Rollie and sprang back.

"Hey, Prof!" a familiar voice greeted.

Mr. Chad bounded into the classroom, his hands stuck casually in his pockets, his blue eyes twinkling.

Professor Enches stumbled back a few steps, bumping into his desk. He fished out a handkerchief from his back pocket and dabbed his brow. As he cleared his throat, he righted his askew tie.

Rollie slumped in his chair, panting. A wave of relief and a warmth of comfort flooded his body as Mr. Chad nonchalantly intervened. When Mr. Chad planted himself next to Rollie, there was no doubt in Rollie's heart regarding Mr. Chad's true blue blood. Relief turned to gratitude, gratitude that Mr. Chad was innocent, gratitude that he had interrupted, and gratitude that, above all, he was an adult.

"Mr. Permiter, now is not a good time," Professor Enches huffed.

"Where's your class?" Mr. Chad asked, surveying the empty room.

Enches cleared his throat impatiently. "Is there something you need?"

"Yes!" Mr. Chad snapped his fingers. "Have you seen my parasol?"

"I beg your pardon! Your what?"

"My parasol," the American shrugged. "I need it for Holmes' old lady disguise."

Enches threw up his hands in irritation. "Do you see a parasol about my person? How absurd!"

"Wait! I remember where I last had it. In Headmaster's office. Rollie, be a sport and go get it for me." Mr. Chad socked Rollie's shoulder playfully.

The professor stiffened. "Rollie is not dismissed yet."

"I'll wait till he is."

"Our conversation is strictly between Rollie and myself."

Mr. Chad leaned in toward his colleague. "Ya know, Prof, it's bad etiquette to show favoritism to one student. Don't get me wrong, Rollie's a great kid, but we're not supposed to play favorites."

Professor Enches reddened, with frustration or embarrassment— it was hard to tell.

"Go on, Rollie. Remember, my parasol is in *headmaster's office*." Mr. Chad discreetly winked. As Rollie stood, Mr. Chad gripped his shoulder warmly and whispered, "I've got this, go!"

Wasting no time, Rollie darted out the classroom and bounded downstairs. He pounded on the headmaster's office door. He hoped Yardsly was back from his errands.

"ENTER!"

Rollie barged in. "Headmaster, Mr. Chad's got him! Hurry, before he gets away! He knows that I know!"

"ROLLIN! What on earth are you talking about?" Yardsly asked as he shot to his feet behind his desk. "CALM YOURSELF! What do you need to tell me?"

Rollie swallowed and collected his thoughts. "I think I know who the thief is, sir."

The headmaster's eyebrows shot up. "DO TELL."

Rollie quickly related his investigation, including his night escapade in the library, his discovery of the disguise in Enches's desk, and his suspicion of the letters he delivered.

When he was finished, headmaster replied, "If what you say is true—about the letter being the final evidence—then I am sorry you were caught this morning."

Rollie allowed a small smile as he pulled the thick parchment envelope out from under his shirt. "I'm not, Headmaster."

*　　　　*　　　　*　　　　*

That evening while everyone ate supper, the headmaster summoned Rollie to his office. All day Rollie had kept quiet about his involvement and kept his questions to himself. He did not want to bother the headmaster about the case. The faculty had been occupied with Enches' arrest instigated by Mr. Chad. Still he wanted to know how the puzzle pieces fit together.

With a flutter of excitement, he skipped downstairs to the headmaster's office. He entered quietly.

"Rollin, my dear detective, take a seat." Headmaster Yardsly waved to the left armchair in front of the crackling fireplace.

Rollie eased into the worn but comfy armchair, remembering Watson always sat on the left. He felt privileged to sit in Dr. Watson's chair.

"I suppose you'd like to know exactly what you were on to, am I right?"

Rollie nodded. "If I'm not allowed to, I understand."

"Well, my little sleuth." The headmaster paused dramatically, and shouted, "YOU DID IT!"

"I solved the library burglary?"

"Yes, and more. It was very brave of you to post yourself in the library. Why did you decide to do that?"

"Because of my marmalade jar, sir. I figured out how to use it in the library. I also figured whoever stole my jar had broken in before."

"You were correct. Ichabod needed your jar to open the secret library."

"He wanted our Sherlock Holmes' volumes, right?"

Headmaster Yardsly tapped his nose knowingly. "And a lot more. Rest assured, Ichabod has been descreetly arrested and is being interrogated by Scotland Yard. GOOD WORK! Does that clear everything up?"

Just like at orientation months ago, there were still lots of unanswered questions in Rollie's head. "Not everything. Why are our books kept in the secret library?"

"A profile of each student is kept in his or her personal volume. That profile includes personal information like home address and IQ scores. More importantly, we hold profiles on past students who are currently serving their country as bobbies, detectives, and spies. All crucial information that could endanger us if it fell into the wrong hands. The wrong hands in this case are Ichabod's."

"What was he going to do with our information?"

"Give it away."

"To whom?"

"That answer was in the letter you delivered from Mr. Crenshaw. My sis—er, Ms. Yardsly worked hard to decode it. Turns out that your neighbor Mr. Crenshaw is the illusive Herr Zilch."

"Herr Zilch? Who's he?"

"A German spy who for many years has worked to dismantle Sherlock Academy and stop our students from becoming detectives. Herr Zilch is the latest leader of a secret organization known as M.U.S."

"I recognize those initials!" Rollie exclaimed. "On the envelopes I delivered. Cecily and I use to spy on Mr. Crenshaw. We saw all kinds of notes and invoices with M.U.S."

"Hmm, spying on your neighbors? Reminds me of when I was a boy…" Yardsly trailed off with a far-away look in his eyes. He snapped his attention back to Rollie and cleared his throat. "M.U.S. stands for Moriarty's Underground Society. Professor Moriarty founded this secret society. I assume you're familiar with him."

"Of course, sir! He was Holmes' greatest nemesis of all time. He was called the Napoleon of crime. Holmes actually respected him because he was so brilliant."

"EXACTLY! He was Holmes' evil competition."

"I can't believe he still has followers! So Herr Zilch wanted those profiles so he could…" Rollie trailed off, not wanting to speak of the horrible reason.

Headmaster Yardsly nodded. "It turns out that Ichabod was Herr Zilch's inside accomplice. They communicated only through letters because Scotland Yard monitors all mail, telegrams, and telephone calls here—we're always on guard against Herr Zilch. But he found a private courier for his letters. "

Rollie adopted a horrified expression. "Me! I was helping them all along!"

"Calm yourself, lad. You had no idea. They were using you, yes, but that turned out to be a lucky tool. Don't blame yourself for any of their crimes," Headmaster Yardsly said firmly.

Rollie nodded. "Yes, sir. Has Herr Zilch been arrested?"

The headmaster rubbed his eyes wearily. "Yet again he evades us. By the time Scotland Yard got to his house, Herr Zilch had evacuated. He may still be in England, or he may have fled back to Germany. But his house has been confiscated, so at least he won't be returning to it. You may get some new neighbors soon."

"He just moved in last Christmas."

"Well, he's been our nemesis for as long as I can remember. All that matters at the moment is that the secret library is safe, Ichabod Enches the accomplice has been arrested, and you are the school hero."

"Hero?"

Headmaster Yardsly reached down beside his chair and brought up a box. He dropped it on Rollie's lap. "For you, in appreciation for your services and to remind you that you're a fine detective."

With excited fingers, Rollie pried the lid off. He took out a plaid felt hat with earflaps tied on the top. It resembled the hat all the illustrations showed Sherlock Holmes wearing. He put it on; a perfect fit.

"Usually we award these deerstalker hats to upperclassmen who solve fieldwork cases. But you've earned it. Just don't flaunt it," Headmaster Yardsly commented with a wink.

"Thank you, sir, thank you very much."

"One thing, Rollie, and I am sorry to require this of you. Our conversation here today must be kept a secret."

"Please may I tell my friend Cecily? She helped me get the letter. She knows everything up to this point. She's my Watson, after all."

Headmaster Yardsly considered. "VERY WELL. Only your Watson, no one else."

As Rollie adjusted the hat on his head, a thought sparked. "Mr. Cren—I mean, Herr Zilch said his nephew used to go here."

Headmaster nodded gravely. "I'd rather not discuss the past."

"One thing I've been wondering, if all our books are safe behind the bookcases, then why—"

"Why the rearranging library?" Headmaster Yardsly chuckled, a mischievous glimmer in his eyes. "A safety diversion. Remember, appearances can be deceiving." He beamed, and added, "Honestly, it's great fun watching students pull their hair out over it!"

"I have another question, sir."

"One more, then off to supper."

"What did the letter say exactly? Or can you not tell me?"

"I'd like to tell you, Rollie, but I must meet with my staff first. There are a few things we need to discuss before I share that with you. I hope they'll agree to tell you."

"Yes, sir." Smiling, Rollie jumped to his feet and bounded to the door. He paused and turned, remembering something. "Ichabod took one of the Sherlock Holmes books when he broke in!"

"No need to worry. We recovered it from his desk. It's safe and sound in the secret library again. I've also taken the liberty of locking up your marmalade jar with mine. Better safe than sorry."

Rollie nodded. "Whose book did Enches take?"

Headmaster Yardsly pursed his thin lips. "Yours."

"Mine?"

"Quite ironic that you were the one to solve the mystery and save the book, being that it was yours."

"I'm glad I did then."

"So am I."

Rollie shuffled his feet uneasily. "Why did he take *my* book?"

"I'm not entirely sure, Rollie, just as I'm not sure why he chose you to deliver his letters. It's no coincidence. Apparently you're someone worth keeping an eye on."

CHAPTER 19

Elementary

When Headmaster Yardsly gave that deerstalker hat to Rollie, he did not make life easier for the boy. Naturally everyone wanted to know why Rollie had been given the hat. The short answer he gave was "It was a thank-you gift for helping him with a problem." That answer only led to more questions, usually ending with why Ichabod Enches had left the academy. Rollie endured this for about a week. By Thursday the students grew bored with the whole thing and gave up pestering Rollie. Except for Eliot.

"Can you get me one of those hats, ol' bean?" he asked while the two boys finished their math homework after supper Thursday evening. Eliot consented to studying with Rollie in the evenings, since he kept falling asleep at dawn.

Ignoring his roommate, Rollie finished his long division.

"Did you hear me?" Eliot persisted.

"Yes, but the answer is no."

"Then tell me how to get one. What kind of problem do I need to help with?"

Rollie erased his answer. He had divided wrong. "I'm not sure. Just keep your eyes open for problems, I guess."

"I need more details, you know? Personal problems with the headmaster? Or maintenance problems with the building? Which reminds me. Our faucet is dripping. If there's one thing I can's stand it's a dripping faucet. All I hear is drip, drip, drip, drip, drip—"

"And all I can hear is yack, yack, yack from my roomie."

"Sorry, chum, but it really annoys me. And I won't rest till it's fixed, or till I get one of those—"

Rollie tossed the hat to him. "You can wear it for the evening. But I better see it back on my bedpost tomorrow morning. Understand?"

"Got it. No worries." Eliot adjusted it on his head and went to the bathroom to admire it in the mirror. "I think it's more becoming on me."

"Of course you do," Rollie muttered with a smile. He did not mind sharing his hat with Eliot. Rollie figured it kept himself from getting too stuck up. There had been moments during the week when he felt a little proud of himself. Everyone else was proud of him, even his family. When the school had notified the family of his heroic deeds, they had sent a congratulatory reply. Rollie's confidence as a detective had boosted, which was a good thing, as long as it did not go too far. He was careful to guard himself against haughtiness.

"Headmaster Yardsly needs to see you right away," a drab voice announced.

Rollie looked up to see his other roommate Rupert standing in the doorway. "Thanks, Rupert."

"I don't need your thanks." Rupert shuffled to his bed and plopped down.

Rollie dashed out the room and down the hall. On the stairs he bumped into Cecily.

"Hey there, big detective, where ya going?"

"Headmaster Yardsly wants to see me. I hope he's going to tell me what's in that letter."

"Ooo, me too! Meet me here when you're done. I'll be waiting." Cecily took a seat on a step.

"Sure thing." Rollie bounded away. When he got to the office, he found not only Headmaster Sullivan P. Yardsly waiting for him behind his desk, but all the other teachers seated in chairs set in a half circle facing the desk. One chair remained empty next to Ms. Yardsly. Rollie assumed the chair was for him and sat down.

"GOOD EVENING, Rollie," the headmaster boomed in his familiar but always alarming way. (He made everyone jump.) "We just concluded our staff meeting and want to share something with you." Yardsly held up a sheet of paper. "Yes, this is the letter. The reason we've agreed to tell you more about this letter is we believe you may be helpful to us. You've proven yourself very helpful with this case. We'd like you to continue developing your detective skills by assisting us with a new mystery."

"I will definitely help you with whatever you want, sir." Rollie quickly glanced around the circle of teachers.

Ms. Katherine E. Yardsly nodded curtly, Miss Amelia S. Hertz giggled, Mr. Percy E. Notch blinked behind his thick glasses, and Mr. Chadwick A. Permiter gave him a thumbs-up.

"WELL THEN! I won't read you the letter—it's quite boring and explains what we already know about Herr Zilch. Based on the other letters from Herr Zilch and a thorough investigation of Ichabod's desk, conducted by Ms. Yardsly and Miss Hertz—thank you, ladies—" He nodded appreciatively at the two teachers. Ms. Yardsly nodded back, and Miss Hertz blushed. "I am relieved to report that no other student books were taken besides yours. However, Enches' interrogation revealed that Herr Zilch still has plans for Sherlock Academy. Wicked plans, mind you."

All eyes turned to Rollie, who did not know how to react.

"Do you know what that means, Rollie?" Headmaster Yardsly asked.

"It means we're still in danger?"

"Perhaps. It could mean anything." The headmaster threw up his hands in clear frustration. "I wanted you to know this so you could help us watch over the academy."

"Be on your guard, Rollin E. Wilson," Ms. Yardsly drilled in her commanding voice.

"Watch out for any prints!" Miss Hertz bubbled.

"Keep your eyes and ears open, except when you're sleeping, of course, or you'll never get any rest," Mr. Notch rambled.

"Be yourself, kid," Mr. Chad said with a wink. "No pressure, or anything," he added jokingly.

"That's all, Rollie. Oh, and you can tell your Watson, but no one else." Headmaster Yardsly shook hands with the boy before he left.

"So? What was in the letter?"

Rollie nearly tripped over Cecily on the stairs before he noticed her. He sunk down beside her. "Cecily, this is top secret."

"I'm your Watson. I'll keep your secret."

Rollie lowered his voice to a whisper, hardly audible. Cecily had to lean in when he said, "Headmaster didn't read me the letter, but he said they've been investigating all the other letters and stuff left by Professor Enches. He thinks that Herr Zilch still has plans for Sherlock Academy."

Cecily stared at him, alarm showing in her green eyes.

Rollie continued. "The teachers want us to help watch over the school. I think they're afraid Herr Zilch will show up again."

Cecily sighed. "Another mystery."

"Well, that's what we enrolled for. Can you believe it's only been three weeks of school and already we've solved a mystery? A real mystery this time."

"We're detectives after all." Cecily paused and shyly bit her lip. "Rollie?"

"Hmm?"

"What you did was very brave. I would have been terrified to face Professor Enches alone."

"I was," Rollie admitted. "I was relieved when Mr. Chad came to the rescue. What a lucky break!"

Cecily smiled. "That wasn't luck—that was me. I told him what happened."

Rollie stared at her with admiration. "See? I knew I needed my Watson."

Cecily nodded and reached down to cuff up her trousers.

"Are those your brother's trousers?"

"Of course. How did you deduce that, Holmes?"

Rollie grinned. "Elementary, my dear Watson!"

About the Author

F.C. Shaw started writing and illustrating stories when she was eight years old. She began with a spiral notebook, moved onto her grandmother's Word Processor, and finally landed on a laptop. She lives with her husband in a home they have ambitiously dubbed *The Manor* in Santa Maria, California. When she's not plotting stories, she teaches visual and performing arts in local schools and enjoys a good game of Scrabble.

Check out
www.sherlockacademy.com